the Roommate Mistake

ALSO BY ELIZABETH STEVENS

the **Roommate**

Mistake

ELIZABETH STEVENS

SLEEPING DRAGON BOOKS
ADELAIDE

Sleeping Dragon Books

the Roommate Mistake
by Elizabeth Stevens

Print ISBN: 978-1925928570
Digital ISBN: 978-1925928563

Cover art by: Izzie Duffield

Copyright 2018 Elizabeth Stevens

Worldwide Electronic & Digital Rights
Worldwide English Language Print Rights

Another one for Andy.
To being friends first, and always.
Maybe you'll read this one :P

Contents

Author's Note

Please, please note that this book is a work of parodical meta fiction, intended to be taken lightly. It revels in the ridiculousness of its situations and well as basks in the absurdity of its plot. Tropes have been taken to the extreme for comedic effect, fully knowing that's what they're there for. Please read this tongue-in-cheek tale with a grain of salt.

I have taken a few liberties in regards to Australian driving laws to make the story work better, choosing to use the Learner system I got my license under a million years ago, rather than how it is now.

This book is written using Australian English. This will affect the spelling, grammar and syntax you may be used to. It might come across as typos, awkward sentences, poor grammar, or missed/wrong words. In the majority of cases (I won't claim it's infallible, despite all best efforts), this is intentional and just an Aussie way of speaking (it took my US beta readers a bit to get used to). I can't say 'the' Aussie way, since we seem to differ even within the same state. Just think of us as a weird mix of British and US vernacular and colloquialisms, but with our own randomness thrown in. I still hope you enjoy it, though!

Chapter One

No one likes moving schools. It sucks. It especially sucks when it's a boarding school. And it most epically sucks when it's at the behest of the grandparents you hate, who insist it's what your dead dad wanted.

Like he'd rather me shipped across the state instead of staying with my friends.

But Mum wasn't one to pass up the opportunity, or my grandparents covering the unnecessarily exorbitant fees.

At least she was making the five-hour drive with me. All the better to remind me why this was a good idea.

"You're a legacy," she was reminding me as she peered over the steering wheel, on the lookout for street signs among the vastness of Australian bush that spread on as though forever.

"That'll come in handy for all those clubs I won't be joining," I answered, my own eye scanning for landmarks the school had assured us existed. I pointed up ahead. "There."

"Thanks," Mum said as she started breaking to take the dirt track off the highway. "I don't want you just sitting in your room for the next two years, doing nothing and not making any friends."

"But I like doing nothing and not making friends," I fake-whined. "Besides I won't be doing nothing. I'll read or game or, God forbid, do my homework on time."

Mum chuckled, then threw me as stern a frown as she could. "I'm serious, though. You have to join something. A club. A team. The Introverts United Guild. Literally anything so I know you're not totally alone here."

"So, we're admitting this is just for you."

She nodded. "It's all for me. My peace of mind."

We were on the driveway now. Although, driveway was a rather lacking word for the track that wound through the muted green-grey foliage that surrounded us. Dappled sunlight flickered over the car as Mum made her way cautiously along.

"Okay, I can guarantee I'll join something."

"There needs to be at least two members."

I slunk down in my seat, grumbling to myself about how well she knew me.

Not for long, though.

The trail we were crawling along finally broke free of the undergrowth and trees the place was named for, and the great big main building – mansion, more like – rose up out of the scrubby grass to greet us.

Acacia Academy.

The country's foremost boarding school. A place for those people, who lived too far away from the main cities, to send their kids even further away. Or a status symbol. A place that was supposed to spit out more elites than a country this size rightly knew what to do with. CEOs. Pioneers. Geniuses. Politicians. Top athletes. Award-winners. Artists. Australia's crème de la crème.

There was a part of me that appreciated and looked forward to joining them, to becoming an Acacia graduate. As much as I might not have cared for my grandparents' snooty ways and snobbery, this would at least be a benefit to me in the long run. One presumed.

"There it is," Mum said reverently, pulling up alongside a whole bunch of other cars with equally stunned-looking children getting out along-side bored parents.

We'd been told the new intake outside Year Eight was miniscule, so it didn't surprise me that new kids in other years were given what appeared to be star treatment of being welcomed through the front doors of the main building when the rest of the students would start to arrive around the back in a couple of hours' time.

"Okay," Mum said as she pulled one of my suitcases out of the boot. "So, the welcome pack said we go in there to be greeted in the hall.

I better-shouldered my satchel and took control of that suitcase so Mum could get the second one out.

"Okay," I said absently.

I was looking around at the other kids getting out of cars. I was easily the oldest new kid. Despite my grandparents' assurances that Year Eleven was a typical ingress point. Despite the fact I was probably one of the shortest – which said little about me and a lot about them. Despite the fact they all looked like they already fit in and

I'd just tripped on the tiniest pebble. I just knew I was the only new kid in my year.

"This is gonna be fun," I muttered as Mum and I battled the gravelly carpark to get to the main building.

"What?" Mum asked.

I shook my head. "Nothing."

We walked into the building to be met by the greeters. All of them were dressed in pale green shirts with the Acacia Academy logo, khaki pants, and brown shoes. There were ten of them. One for each of us new kids. Plastered on their faces like they'd be whipped otherwise were giant, welcoming grins.

"Elliott Hopkins?" one of them asked me and Mum.

We nodded.

"Yes," Mum said. "This is Elliott. I'm Mary."

The greeter shook both our hands, directing all conversation to Mum. "Welcome to Acacia. We're thrilled to have Elliott with us. We'll send your bags on to your room, and I'll give you the tour."

I was starting to feel overwhelmed. Not just from the pressure of starting in a new place, but from the sudden realisation of exactly what I was supposed to live up to.

The entry hall was wood panelled in some rich-coloured timber. There were trophies and shields and portraits everywhere, showcasing the achievements of prestigious alumni. I felt the weight of it, but I was also hopeful that it was at least a good place to stoke my passion for knowledge.

Already, I could picture my own little nook of the library where I could study to my heart's content. It went a long way to easing the sudden pressure and overwhelmed sensation.

"Leave your bags with us, and I'll show you around."

I trailed around the school after the greeter and Mum, trying to remember where and what everything was. I had my campus map in my hands, aiming to follow our progress, but I got distracted by the sheer size of everything, the level of tech. Each classroom we passed had two smartboards, surrounded by a modern chic glass architecture. The Hall would hold twice the size of my previous school easily. Even the dining hall looked like it belonged in some early 2000s movie with its surprising space and taste.

I found myself back at the entry hall to the main

building and couldn't remember what we'd just been shown.

"So, usually at this point," the greeter was saying, "parents head off and we let the students get settled in."

Mum let out a big breath. "Okay." She nodded. "No. Okay. I can… We can do that, can't we?"

I smirked at her. "You can't change your mind now. It's way too late."

Mum put her arm around my shoulder and pulled me close. "I'm not changing my mind."

We'd had this conversation at home the night before. The 'I'm going to miss you, but this will be good for you' conversation. We'd got all the feelings out over lots of chocolate and pizza. But that didn't mean that we didn't have a bit of an emotional goodbye before I waved her back off down the long driveway.

With nothing but my satchel and phone for familiar company, I looked around and wondered what to do. First things first seemed to be to see if I could find my dorm again on my own. It took me almost half an hour – most of that was just getting around the giant campus – but I finally managed it. I wasted another couple of hours unpacking the essentials I was going to need for the start of the year on Wednesday.

My dorm allocation info told me my roommate was one Sasha Landry, but there was no sign of her yet. Her door was closed so I didn't know if she'd even arrived or not. It wasn't like I minded putting off meeting new people for a little bit longer.

After that, there was still a bit of time before dinner, so what else was a girl to do but find the all-important library. It had been a major selling point for me. One of the main reasons I'd given in when Mum first told me my grandparents expected me to go to my dad's old school. They'd shown me a picture of it and I'd fallen in love. All that was left was to actually live it in person.

Finding it was easier said than done.

I must have walked around for over an hour. In and out of buildings. Up and down stairs. Navigating my way around more and more students as the time passed.

I saw the crowd parting up ahead of me. It wasn't normally something I'd notice, but I was on the lookout for signage after all, so my eyes weren't trained on the ground in front of my feet the way they usually were.

Emerging from the crowd were five boys.

It was like one of those slow-motion scenes out of a movie.

Front and centre was clearly the leader of the pack. One of those 'hottest guy in school' types. Backed up by the way other kids ogled him as he passed them.

He was tall I guess, but not enough to be ridiculous. He had dark hair, all up and to one side like it was some sort of unconscious tick of his to train it that way. He strode with the easy confidence of the inherently popular, that commanding presence that said he owned these hallways. Even from a distance, and not that it was turned anywhere near me, I could see the cocky smirk playing at his lips. It grew as he surveyed his kingdom and there went his hand through his hair, like he was making sure it stayed in the position he clearly spent a lot of time perfecting.

Mr It was flanked by the required best mates to make up their little popular a-hole clique. The big blond like some kind of Viking had fallen into the wrong century. The shorter red-head in the stripey t-shirt. The tall, lanky one with the dark blond hair. And the slightly leaner one with the light brown hair. Between them, they ticked all the stereotypical boxes that made up high school.

Nothing about them, as easy on the eyes as they may have been, was my type. The constant humour on their faces, like everyone and everything was a huge joke. The air of haughty better-than-you-ness that wafted off of them in waves that befitted a stormy sea. The hint of what would, in a few more years of effortless work, be rippling muscles that denoted the sporty. The general look of basic airheaded blankness that made me think there wasn't a lot going on between their ears.

I went back to my search for the library, determined to find it by my own devices.

If I was in the right place, then the library was supposed to be…

"Right here…?" I muttered to myself.

I paused in the corridor to get my bearings. With my nose buried in my campus map, naturally I caused someone to bump into me. The someone just happened to be Mr It. Of course.

"You right, newbie?" he chuckled.

I looked up at him and felt the vague stirrings of appreciation that he was clearly anticipating. Shame that my brain was perfectly in control and I didn't fall for it just because it was expected of me.

"Yeah. Sorry," I said, side-stepping to get out of his way, which was, in his defence, the middle of the corridor.

"Only be sorry if you won't tell me your name," he said, all smooth and casual flirtation like it was the only language he spoke.

I looked up at him through my eyelashes, feeling my heated look was more incredulous glare than it was flirty desire. I blinked once. "Does that usually work?" I asked.

He also blinked, but his confusion was tinged with impressed humour. "It's never failed me yet."

"Good for you," I told him and at least two of his friends sniggered.

Mr It didn't let my lack of awe put him off his game. "You need someone to…show you around, you let me know." He gave me a cheeky little wink.

I looked him over. "Helpful."

He shrugged with a sort of disingenuous modesty. "It's my pleasure."

I locked my eyes with him. "I don't doubt it."

By the way his friends reacted, my intended burn

11

landed with a perfect ten out of ten. Mr It's eyes were laughing too, even if his smirk was half-incredulity. He sucked his teeth and nodded.

"All right, then," he semi-chuckled. "Fair play. Can I at least aim your self-respect towards a particular destination?"

I felt my eyes narrow, trying to deduce if he was actually trying to be helpful now. "I'm looking for the library…" I said slowly.

His eyes scanned me from toe to top and I saw the lightbulb go off in his head: red alert; this girl isn't your type. I saw his body language change. He was still cocky and flirty – clearly that was his default – but he wasn't trying anything on now.

"Up one more floor," he said, pointing to the ceiling. "Otherwise, you're in the right place."

I spared a look for his friends, then gave him a nod of thanks. "Cheers."

"No problem."

Mr It and I exchanged a glance for a heartbeat longer than I thought was strictly necessary, but there was something odd in it. Not like some lingering look you shared with the guy you crushed massively on while he was all oblivious. Not like the one you shared with the guy who you knew liked you but you were way too awkward to do anything about it.

For a second, I half-entertained the idea of what dating him would be like. For half a second, I saw what it would be like and there was something vaguely intriguing about it. Then, the moment was over and I was more than happy to go on my way and let him go on his.

Chapter Two

I woke up the next morning with a sense of ennui hanging over me. I didn't hate being at Acacia. I wasn't chomping at the bit to run away home. I didn't feel lonely or abandoned or anything. I just felt meh about it.

Meh seemed to sum up a significant portion of my life to date. I'd never been the kind to get all involved in everything. I was the sideliner, content to watch other people live their lives. I'd never known why. There wasn't some tragedy in my past that made me too scared to live life to the fullest. There wasn't some second-hand stressor that had me afraid of being hurt. It was just me. As an only child, I was used to and happy with my own company. I preferred books to people, and I supposed I preferred people to loneliness.

Still, I'd promised Mum that I'd try to make friends so, when I heard movement outside my door, I decided I should probably introduce myself to my roommate who I'd yet to see. Not surprising really considering I'd been investigating, eating, or tucked away in my room.

Which was fine as far as rooms go. There was a bed, bedside table, desk and chair, chest of draws, some hanging space, and a laundry basket with a bag tagged with 'Room 605'. It would suit my purposes fine. There were power points and lamps, so my reading and recharging were sorted.

By the time I dragged myself out of bed, dressed, and into the common living room both bedrooms shared, there was no sign of my roommate. Her door was closed like it had been every time I'd seen it. I looked around at the place I was calling home for basically the next two years.

There was a couch, a couple of chairs, a large TV with console next to it, and a coffee table. On one side of the room was a tiny kitchenette. More a few cupboards that had been turned into a kitchenette. Big enough for a kettle, microwave and toaster; things we'd need for a snack between meals. On the other wall was a big window complete with a cushy window seat. It overlooked the back of the school so there was just scrub and bushland, green even for the time of year.

Since I was up and had very little else to do, I decided more exploring was in order. I wasn't a breakfast person. Never had been. I downed a cup of tea and orange juice while pulling some clothes on as best I could. But, then, there was only so much exploring even I could do. With the knowledge I was stuck here for two years, I wasn't all that keen to uncover all its secrets quite so soon. So, back to my dorm it was.

"Uh, hi…" I said as I walked in and saw the guy standing in the living room, looking at the phone in his hand.

It was Mr It.

It was Mr It in nothing but a low-slung towel.

He turned and looked me over. "Newbie," he said with a smug smile and some admittedly very fine abs on display; a very definite four-pack and a six-pack threatening.

I looked around the room. Presumably Mr It was

Sasha's boyfriend or…boy toy at least. I was sort of impressed with her without even meeting her if the girl's having half naked guys wander around our dorm when the dorm mistress could walk in at any moment.

"You lost?" he asked, making it sound like he was a breath away from some joke about being the one to find me.

I looked at the door and checked it was the right number. "I don't think so."

He nodded, still looking amused. "All right then."

Before he could make a quip about being the right guy in the right place, I got to the point. "I'm looking for–"

"I'm Alex." He still wore that smug grin and I couldn't be sure, but I think he was flexing his pecs.

I nodded. "Great. I'm Lottie–"

"Now you give me your name?" he laughed.

"Sure. Uh, is…" I looked around again. "Sasha…around?" I looked up at him and there was a touch of confusion marring that smugness.

"How do you…?" he spluttered, seeming to be forcing that smile. "Who gave you that name?" he asked.

I went to pull a wad of papers out of my pocket, because

I carried around stuff like that. "My dorm allocation paper says my roommate's name is Sasha…?"

I heard him scoff and I looked up. "So…" A pause. "Please tell me Lottie's short for…Charlotte?" he asked, running his hand over his chin thoughtfully.

I scoffed as I looked through the papers. "Um. No. Lottie's short for Elliott. I'm Elliott Hopkins."

He pointed at me and I don't think he could decide if he was worried about something or he was going to laugh. "*You're* Elliott…?"

I nodded. "Yes."

"*You're–*"

"My name isn't going to change the more you say it," I told him. I looked around. "Where's Sasha? Maybe she can–?"

"He."

I blinked. "What?"

"I'm Sasha."

"You said you were Alex."

A shrug. "People call me Alex."

I frowned. "But…you're a guy."

"That I am. Elliott's a dude's name, isn't it?"

18

"So, what does that make Sasha?"

"Russian."

"Russian?"

He nodded. "My mother's family were Russian. She named me after her grandfather. But here, I'm Alex."

"Oh." I supposed that made sense. "So, you're... You're Sasha Landry?"

He nodded. "And you're Elliott Hopkins."

"So, we're..." I started.

"Roommates," he finished with me.

We sized each other up. I was well aware that he found me as lacking as I found him. What I didn't know what who was at the disadvantage with him being half-naked. By all accounts, what he had on display was impressive enough. If you liked that sort of thing. He was still half-naked and therefore vulnerable. Then again, I got to look at it.

I could just see myself in his eyes: shoulder-length auburn hair with a high probability of messy curls, a button up shirt and pressed culottes, and tennis shoes. I was the aging librarian well before my time, but with a hint of grunge.

I watched him rub his hand over his chin.

He nodded. "Right. Well, I guess we should mention this to someone?"

I also nodded. "I suppose so. Can't imagine the establishment will be terribly pleased if they discover this little mess and we said nothing."

Alex inclined his head. "No. Shame. True. Just let me get dressed and we'll go find the dorm mistress."

"You know where her office is?"

He smirked. "Oh, yeah. I know where her office is."

As he walked into his room, I wondered why that sounded an awful lot like he'd been there a lot? Probably for doing things in his dorm he wasn't supposed to. I didn't need to dwell on it too long, as he was back and thankfully fully dressed in moments. Simple jeans and a t-shirt combo that somehow still looked like it cost an arm and a leg.

As he passed the mirror outside his door, he ran his hand through and up his hair. That mannerism was going to become too familiar much too quickly for my liking.

"Come on, then," he said and I followed him out into the hallway.

It was swarming with kids coming and going. People –

20

kids, teachers, and miscellaneous – called out greetings to him as we passed them. He waved at the ones further away, fist bumped the ones closer, and cracked a smile at every single one of them like he was dousing them in the high beams of his personality.

"Yo, Lando!" someone called out and I saw two boys heading towards us through the crowded hallway.

Alex kicked his chin at them. It was the tall, dark blond and the short red-head from the day before.

"Birdman. Zachary." The three of them shook hands and embraced.

"You got yourself a shadow already, mate?" the short red-head chuckled, looking at me.

Alex laughed. "Nah. Dorm mistress cocked up. Fellas, this is Elliott Hopkins, my roommate."

"For now," I said with a frown.

The tall one smirked, looking at Alex knowingly. "Sure. Nice to meet you…*Elliott*?"

My frown deepened. "He gets to be Sasha and I don't get to be Elliott?"

Red-head held up his hands defensively and tried hard not to smile. "Because the only one allowed to call him

21

Sasha is his grandma, and even then she gets a death glare."

I looked at Alex, finding that a very interesting tid-bit of information indeed.

"Well, if you'll excuse us…*Birdman*," I said wryly, one thin brown eyebrow rising. The one that was pierced. "But *Sasha* and I need to clean up a mess."

The boys shared a smirk.

"That we do," Alex told him.

The tall one laughed. "First girl I've ever seen other than Babushka who's ever told him what to do."

"Don't read into it," Alex warned him.

They shared another handshake and Alex waved his hand to me to follow him.

"So, you're a popular jerkwad then?" I asked and he looked back to her with a laugh.

"There are worse people for a newbie to be stuck with for a roomie, *Elliott*," he replied.

"Sure, *Sasha*," I scoffed. "Lucky me."

He huffed a laugh as smiled at some people, then turned to me. "You some kind of snob there, Elliott?"

"No more than you, I'll bet."

"And what does that mean?"

"Merely, Sasha, that it's not lost on me that you're only talking to me because I have boobs."

"Why? Because I'm some popular arsehole who hates women unless some part of them is wrapped around my cock?" he scoffed.

"You're just that sort. Your kind don't talk to mine."

"Oh, and you think you know my kind do you?" he chuckled.

I nodded resignedly. "I know your kind."

He paused and looked me over like he was trying to work out what in the hells that sentence was supposed to mean. More worryingly, it seemed like he knew what it meant and was debating the sense in digging further into that. Thankfully, he didn't. Instead, he just turned to the next door along the corridor.

"Here it is." Alex knocked on the door to the dorm mistress' office.

For the day before the first official day back, the poor woman already looked overwhelmed. Papers and folders were all over her desk, her hair had fly-aways, and her expression was one of the epically lost.

She looked up and our presence seemed to stress her out further. "Yes?"

"You're new," Alex said, like it was a surprise.

"I am," she answered, looking none too impressed with him. "I'm sure I'll still be able to help you, though."

"Good. Uh, we have a…" Alex looked at me with an easy, casual smirk, "small problem."

The dorm mistress sighed, but tried to look put-together. "What problem?"

"We've been assigned as roommates," he said.

She looked between us, her gaze finally landing on me. I watched her eyes go from slightly glazed and vacant to wide and full of recognition.

"Elliott Hopkins," the dorm mistress said with a sudden burst of energy.

Alex looked at me, clearly wondering who I was to be recognised by the new dorm mistress of all people. I gave a shrug in his direction. I didn't know why she'd know who I was. I sure didn't recognise her.

"That's me," I said.

She nodded. "Yes, hi. Lovely to meet you in person. I heard about your father. I'm so–"

24

"Thanks," I said loudly, feeling like this popular butthole didn't need to know about my dirty laundry.

Of course the only reason she knew who I was was because of my dad. I had no inclination to ask her how she knew my dad. Anything connecting Elliott Hopkins the elder and Acacia wasn't something I cared to know about.

"And you are?" the dorm mistress asked Alex.

"Who am I?" he asked, legitimately confused that she didn't know who he was.

She nodded as she hunted for something on her desk. "Yes. Who are you?"

"I'm Alex Landry," he said, utterly indignant.

She nodded. "Okay, Alex…" She obviously found the folder she was looking for and opened it. "I have Elliott's roommate down as Sasha Landry." She looked up. "Is that your sister?"

"My sister?"

Alex looked thoroughly exasperated. Based on what little I'd seen of him over the last two days, it was obvious that he was used to everyone knowing who he was in every facet of his life. The fact the new dorm mistress not only didn't know who he was but knew who I was had clearly broken what little brain he had.

The dorm mistress looked at Alex expectantly. "Yes. Your sister?"

"No. Sasha Landry is not my sister. *I'm* Sasha Landry."

The dorm mistress, who finally looked like she had a handle on things, lost said handle. "You said your name was Alex."

"He does that," I told her, kicking my head towards him.

He looked between us. "Seriously? Where's Mrs Richards?"

The dorm mistress shrugged. "I don't know. They didn't tell me. But I'm Miss Fairley and I'm the dorm mistress for Banksia House now. You're telling me you, Alex, are Sasha Landry?"

He nodded. "Yes. I'm Sasha Landry. Anglicised 'Alex'. 605 has been my dorm room for the last three years."

"And yet I…" Miss Fairly muttered to herself as she looked at the papers. "Okay. Well…" she breathed out. "Bugger."

Alex snorted and I felt myself smile.

"Yeah, bugger covers it pretty well," he said. "Now, I

26

don't mind having a chick for a roommate. But, if the dean gets wind of this then, no matter how much money my parents throw at the school, I'm going to get into more trouble than even I can get away with."

Miss Fairly looked up at us and seemed to also have so many questions about that. She didn't ask any of them, though. "The fourth dorm is over schedule for its upgrade as it is, so not only is the other girls' dorm over capacity, but we've also had to accommodate some of the girls here in Banksia. With so little space, it might be a while before we can find you somewhere…more suitable, Elliott."

"Lottie, please," I said automatically; it was like a Pavlovian response with me. "And we're not in a day and age where people of the opposite sex can share a dorm?"

Miss Fairly looked like I'd caught her out on something. Like she wanted to say, were it up to her, it would be fine. What luck there were always higher bodies to dictate what was right or wrong and we didn't have to take any responsibility.

"It's not really appropriate."

"No. Shame I'm not a lesbian. I'm sure it would all be above board then."

27

I heard a snort escape Alex and spared him a glance to find he was desperately trying not to laugh. It lit his eyes up and they didn't look quite so blank and empty anymore.

"Look, for what it's worth," he started. "My parents will definitely sign off on me sharing a dorm with a girl. Especially if it makes things easier. Catch them at the right time and they'll probably throw some money in to help get the upgrades finished."

Miss Farley honestly looked like she wasn't quite sure what she was going to do and that it would be great if the answer to the problem was so simple.

"Lottie? Would your mum sign off?"

I felt my eyes rolling of their own accord. Would the woman who lived like she belonged in the sixties with all their free love but with a truly contemporary open-minded mind-set sign off on me sharing a dorm with a guy? I had little doubt, but she should be the one to make that decision.

"You'd have to ask her," I said.

Miss Fairly nodded. "All right. We'll get in touch with your parents and find a resolution to this as soon as we can. In the meantime, I suppose we have very little option but to send you two back to your room for the night."

"Bold of you, Miss Fairly," Alex teased.

She didn't seem to take the joke well. "I expect you to purport yourself in an appropriate manner in these extenuating circumstances, Mr Landry."

The way she said it was so much like she was trying to pass off any responsibility to whatever she thought we were going to get up to. Like seriously, never in a million years was I going to find myself getting up to anything with Alex Landry that required a closed door.

Not. Going. To. Happen.

Chapter Three

The next morning, the persistent buzz of my phone woke me up. Just because it had been the intention didn't make it any better. With a groan, I rolled myself over and fumbled around under my pillow to find the offending object.

I was well-practiced in the art of silencing my alarm with eyes still full of sleep. However, even still half-asleep – on the verge of being back asleep – I noticed the little notification from the Acacia App.

A mandatory app the school ran, it required a log-in on my part – with credentials passed out by the school – and gave me instant access to everything I might need, catered specifically to me. Timetable. Emails. Class materials.

And the in-school instant messenger system. Why have a boring, simple online portal when you could fashion the whole thing into an exorbitant custom phone app? At least the ridiculous fees weren't just being used for yet another – probably native Australiana-themed – cup for the rugby team or something.

Resignedly awake now, I rolled onto my back and opened the app. There was a message from Miss Fairly to a group which shared the personal contact information of Alex and me with each other.

"Great," I muttered to myself. "Now he can slide into my DMs as well as my room."

Not that Alex had tried sliding into my room.

Miss Fairly – Dorm Mistress, Banksia House

I have set up a meeting with your guardians at 11am this morning. Please come to my office then. I will inform your relevant teachers.

Miss Fairly

I wasn't sure if that was the sort of thing to which one replied. She could see I'd read it; did it need a response? It

31

wasn't like I had a choice in the matter anyway. I had to go.

Didn't stop Alex replying. The small insight into his psyche did nothing to change my opinion of him.

Alex Landry

K

"'K'?" I muttered to myself as I pulled up my keyboard. "Neanderthal."

'K' was the sort of response your technologically challenged grandparents sent you in response to the huge missive of what you'd been up to that week. 'K' was the sort of thing your mum sent when you told her you were on the way home. It was the bare minimum of a reply, not the sort of thing you used in formal school communique.

Elliott Hopkins

Thank you. I will attend your office at

11am today.

Lottie Hopkins

I felt quite pleased with myself as I hit send, then wondered why the hell I'd felt the need to show up Alex in the first place. I just couldn't help it. The guy got under my skin by just existing. The previous afternoon, he'd pestered me about showing me around and meeting some people I might like, and going to the dining hall together. Thankfully, he'd been distracted by the arrival of more of his friends, so I hadn't needed to do any of those things and avoided him successfully.

I'd have to see how successful I'd be for the official first day of Acacia Academy's Term One. Who knew what classes we might have together or, worse yet, homegroup. That was a legitimate concern since I'd read that Acacia's homegroup system was based on dorms and was designed to foster friendships among dormmates. The last thing I needed was friendships, let alone with anyone in my dorm.

"Rise and-or shine, Elliott Hopkins!" I heard through my door. "This is your official welcome to your first day at the excellence that is Acacia Academy."

By the time he'd finished his little spiel, I'd managed to haul arse out of bed and throw my bedroom door open. I didn't need the look on his face to confirm how good I looked first thing in the morning; I knew what I was and future swamp witch was not only an apt title but something I looked forward to.

"What?" I asked, my voice groggy as hell.

But Alex Landry was clearly a morning person.

There he stood with that charming smile beaming at me at about a million lumens. He was already dressed in his full uniform with not a wrinkle out of place. His hair was characteristically pulled up again and, as I waited for some explanation as to why he was at my door so chipper so early, my half-asleep brain watched him half-mesmerised as he ran his hand through and up it again.

"Good morning," he said with a widening of his grin.

"Is it?" I asked.

He nodded. "It is."

"Then go and enjoy it instead of waking me up."

How could his smile get even bigger? How? "Ah, but you replied to Miss Fairley's message, ergo you must have already been awake."

My brain got stuck on marvelling he knew the word 'ergo' and it took a while for it to move onto any other thought. "I can sleep reply. I'm rather proficient at the sleep reply." And I was. Much like, I imagined, any person who hated waking up but was expected to function during society's pre-approved hours of custom.

He seemed to mull it over as his eyes scanned me again.

It was still the height of Australian summer in a building more suited to the rolling green blessed plots of England than the rustling dry scrub of the Australian bush (sure, it looked good, but it stuck out like a sore thumb). Being that it was still so warm out and I was not a Summer creature, I was wearing a tank top and shorts. It was this not terribly concealing get up that his eyes scanned.

They did it with practised simplicity, like it was second nature to judge a young woman's worth by her outsides as you held a fleeting conversation. What better way to keep the conversation brief and get the information you wanted? It wasn't like I hadn't done the exact same thing to him when I opened the door.

To his credit, while he clearly couldn't turn off the easy charmer part of his personality and definitely had some choice quips on the edge of his tongue in regards to my state, he didn't try anything on.

"Not a morning person, then."

I couldn't tell if it was a question or not and, if it was, whether he was asking himself or me.

Either way, I shrugged. "Not. No."

He gave me a nod. "Right. Well. I–"

35

There was a drumming noise from the living room door and a raucously called, "Alex! Alex! Alex!"

Alex smirked like I was joining in on the joke. "I'll leave you to it. See you later?"

Figuring I had no choice but to see him at some point in my day – although it would prove an interesting social experiment to see how long I could avoid him – I nodded. "See you later."

"Alex!" came the call again.

He gave me one more cheerful nod, then headed off to deal with the very loud people at the dorm door. His overly enthusiastic words unintelligible as I turned back into my room, pushing the door closed again with my foot, and tried to remember where I'd put my uniform.

By the time I was dressed and found my school map in the things I'd packed up in preparation for the first day, I just got to Assembly on time. It was longer than usual apparently, covering a whole bunch of details that mostly meant nothing to me as a new student; sports news, club reminders, updates on building works and schemes, tournament announcements, and of course a massive welcome from various members of staff.

Two hours later, it was Recess time. Which was good, because it was about that time of the day that my stomach started thinking it was hungry. It was also good because it was the first time I could walk the halls of Acacia Academy without a map for guidance; everyone else was going to the Dining Hall as well.

The noise of hundreds of moving, chatting, excited students surrounded me. The jostling alone was enough to make me feel like I'd be swallowed up by the flow if I tried to do anything but follow it. There was, though, something wholesome in being surrounded by people genuinely happy to see each other after a long absence.

I was sitting on my own at the end of one of the long wooden tables when a shadow fell across me. Strike that. Multiple shadows.

Great, I thought to myself. *Time for the new kid to be hounded by the popular girls.*

Looking up, I saw it was just Alex. Alex and his friends.

He nodded in greeting, a jut of his chin in my direction. "Hey."

I inclined my head to him. "Hi. Can I help you with something?"

"Thought I'd grab you on the way to Miss Fairley's office."

I looked at the four boys behind him. All in their green and grey uniforms, they looked like they were about to drop some throwback boyband album.

"Did this thought also include your entourage escorting us there?" I asked him.

He huffed a laugh. "Nah. They're just dropping me to you."

"Are you not allowed to go anywhere unaccompanied? Or just incapable?"

One of his friends, the Viking-looking one, sniggered as he elbowed the lean one. "I like her."

I raised my eyebrow as I looked back to Alex, as though he would have any explanation for what was going on.

There was zero need nor want for this giant blond boy to like me. It was bad enough Alex had decided it was fair game to talk to me just because there'd been a bungle about our sexes. Under no other circumstances, in no other universe, would these people be talking to me otherwise. It was a pity.

I looked at the time and saw it was almost eleven. Given

I was still working my way around the school, I probably should have been already on my way. I supposed, this once, having someone talk to me wasn't the worst thing in the world.

"All right. I guess we may as well go to Miss Fairley's office together, then." I stood up and made to pick my tray up.

The short red-head took it from me. "We've got it. You don't want to be late."

I bit back a retort about what he knew about what I didn't and didn't want; I'd learnt that antagonism wasn't always the best policy, especially when these people did seem to be genuinely trying to be nice.

"Uh, thanks." I nodded. "Shall we?" I asked Alex.

He gave me a smile and a nod, said goodbye to his friends, then headed off in a manner that suggested I follow. Follow I did and we came to Miss Fairley's office a mite before eleven and with zero getting lost or turned around.

"Ah, Alex. Lottie," she said when she saw us hovering in the door. "Come in. Come in. We're almost ready. Take a seat."

Alex indicated me towards one chair like he would have pulled it out for me had we been sitting down to eat. I sat in his suggested seat, only because he was standing in the way of the other one.

"Good morning," came a new voice from the doorway.

I turned around a saw a stern-looking woman I recognised from the Acacia brochures. It was the Principal. Tamara Wilson. Newly appointed. First female principal the school had ever had, breaking years of old boys' club tradition. What was she doing here?

"Uh, Ms Wilson," Miss Fairley said, looking around her office in panic like she thought she was about to be told off. "What brings you–"

"I'm here on behalf of my sister," Ms Wilson said as she looked Alex over knowingly. "What has my nephew been up to now?"

Ms Wilson's eyes slid over to me and I saw the exasperation clear as day on her face. I meanwhile was tucking away the tid-bit of information in case it came in handy. Why my brain thought I needed potential blackmail info against Alex, I wasn't sure. It either spoke to who I was as a person or who I assumed he was, and I didn't much care to know which.

"Really, Alex?" Ms Wilson asked, clearly already decided what had happened. "Already? It's *literally* day one."

Alex gave her a grin that was intended to charm the pants off even the strictest of family members. Clearly, Ms Wilson was far more than the strictest of family members.

"Relax," he told her. "No one's been caught doing anything naughty."

Miss Fairley clearly only just realised what Ms Wilson had assumed and went bright red. "Oh. Uh. No," she stammered, blinking furiously behind her glasses. "Mr Landry assured me there would be no…inappropriate shenanigans."

"No," Alex agreed. "I'm a strict 'appropriate shenanigans only' kinda guy."

I rolled my eyes. "There were no shenanigans, appropriate or inappropriate."

Ms Wilson looked at me, looked at Alex, looked at me, then looked at Miss Fairley. "Then why am I here? What meeting is his parents unable to make?"

"Ah, now see…" Miss Fairley started.

41

Alex took over with his suave tone. "An error was made. Lottie and I were assigned as roommates and it looks like finding her a new dorm is going to prove a little tricky."

"I knew Elliott– Lottie's father–" Miss Fairley started by way of apologetic explanation.

Ms Wilson looked at her as she interrupted. "And with 'Sasha' as his official…" She trailed off with a sigh as her gaze returned to her nephew. "That's what this morning's donation was for?"

Alex gave her a shrug. "I assume so."

Ms Wilson sighed heavily. "Yes. Because money will always solve the problem." She sighed again and her attention was back to Miss Fairley. "What can we do?"

Miss Fairley was clearly doing her best 'professional and with it' impression. "As finding Lottie a new room could take a while, it was suggested we would have a meeting with the parents to see if they gave their consent for Lottie and…Alex to share a dorm in the interim."

Ms Wilson almost smiled upon realising that this woman had no idea who her nephew was – versus clearly knowing who I was – and even more so upon seeing how

42

annoyed this made him.

Before she answered, she cleared her throat and the smile was gone. "I see. And Lottie's parents…?"

"About to be on the line now," Miss Fairley said as she did something on her computer.

"So sorry I'm late," I heard Mum's voice play through the speakers.

Miss Fairley nodded to the monitor while giving a side eye to Ms Wilson. "No problem, Mrs Hopkins. I'm here with Lottie, as well as Alex and his…guardian."

She spun the monitor and there was Mum in all her bohemian glory – messy bun, glasses, flowing kaftan, no makeup. They said that if you wanted to know what a woman would look like in 'x' number of years, then look at her mother. If I looked like that in any number of years, then I had an awful lot of changing to do.

"Oh, hi," Mum said, waving to the room. "Nice to meet you, I'm Mary Hopkins, Lottie's mum."

Ms Wilson nodded. "Tamara Wilson. Alex's aunt."

Mum's eyes narrowed as she moved closer to the screen. "Wait. Aren't you the principal?"

Ms Wilson nodded. "I am here, however, in the

capacity of guardian. Alex's mother is my sister."

"Alex Landry, Mary. Pleased to meet you," he said, angling himself better in the camera's scope.

I rolled my eyes. Mum was obviously charmed. "Oh, hello. I hear there's been a bit of a mix up with the dorm allocation?"

"Yes," Ms Wilson said stonily. "I'm afraid we're doing renovations to Callistemon House, so room is…sparse this year. As such we've had to accommodate some of the girls in Banksia House. We appear to have had a confusion as to where Elliott and Sasha belong."

I could see Mum had ideas about 'where I belonged'. Thankfully, she didn't voice them all aloud. "Well, I'm sure these things happen. What do you need from me?"

"Put frankly, Mrs Hopkins, we're not sure when or if we'll be able to find Lottie a new dorm until the renovations are complete," Miss Fairley said, her tone all apology.

Despite her being there in the guardian capacity, Ms Wilson took over. "What we need, Mrs Hopkins, is your permission for Lottie and Alex to continue to share the dorm. They have separate rooms and Miss Fairley will be

44

keeping a close eye on them."

Mum smirked and I was sure she was remembering stories Dad had told about good old Acacia Academy and their success in segregating the sexes. Naturally, he'd not told me any of them directly, but I'd overheard enough to know that allocating the students different dormitories had done very little to keep them out of each other's beds. Teenagers were nothing if not a resourceful bunch when they really wanted something.

"Well, it sounds like I really don't have much choice here," Mum said.

"Rest assured, we are doing everything we can to have the renovations finished and the school back to order," Miss Fairley said.

Mum shrugged. "It honestly makes very little difference to me. If it's permission you need to make yourselves feel better and cover your legal butts, then you've got it."

Miss Fairley looked to Ms Wilson, who sighed.

"As Mrs Hopkins said, we have very little choice. But, Alex, know that you are answerable to me as both principal and aunt here. One wrong step and–"

"Look, no offence, Aunt Tam, but Lottie's not exactly falling over herself to get in my pants and the feeling's mutual. You got nothing to worry about *shenanigans*-wise."

Ms Wilson looked like she was caught between wanting to believe him and wanting to berate him into taking this seriously. I wondered what kind of relationship they had outside of her being the principal.

"Okay," Ms Wilson said. "As Alex's guardian, I also give my permission."

Miss Fairley looked like she was just happy to have the situation out of her hands. "Wonderful. I'll draw up some paperwork to sign and keep you apprised of our efforts to find Lottie a new dorm," she said, more to Mum than Ms Wilson I was sure.

"Excellent. Sounds good," Mum said with a nod. "I'll get right on that." Which was Mary Hopkins code for 'I'll plan to do that, forget for an inordinate amount of time, need ten reminders, then eventually do it when the fates align'.

"Thank you, Mrs Hopkins," Ms Wilson said. "I'm glad we could sort this out quickly and with minimal fuss."

Goodbyes were said, Mum signed off and Alex and I were dismissed.

"What class have you got now?" he asked.

"Maths."

"No way!"

"You have Maths now?" I guessed.

He shook his head. "Nope. Tourism. But! Maths is in the same block. I'll walk you."

"I don't need a chaperone."

"Fine. I'm going to the same building, can I please walk with you?" he asked.

I looked at him and found it very difficult not to smile. "Fine. You can walk with me," I caved.

He grinned. "Awesome."

Later that day, I texted Mum about the absolutely surreal situation I'd found myself in.

Lottie

Well. You wanted me to join something.

Does the circus count?

Mum

LOL!

Mum

No.

To what would be Mum's utter chagrin, I locked myself away in my room and looked up my new roommate.

From what I could gather, Alex Landry had risen to school stardom the year before when he surpassed all previous expectations and smashed every single swimming record the school ever held, both internally and in competitions. It was no wonder people knew who he was.

School newsletters for the past year had at least one mention of him and his accomplishments, if not a whole article. The guy might be arrogant, but at least it seemed somewhat earned. I had to give him that. If my school made such a big deal about me, I'd probably walk around like I owned the place, too.

The introvert and the jock as roommates.

It sounded like the beginning of a really bad joke.

"Well," I muttered to myself. "This year just got a whole lot more interesting."

Chapter Four

My second day at Acacia was no less busy than the first. There was just the added complication of having Alex waiting for me first thing in the morning. At least he hadn't knocked on my door again.

"Here I thought you were gonna miss first lesson," he said, far too chipper for that time of the morning. Worse, his hair was wet like he'd been up long enough to have already showered.

"Why would I miss first lesson?" I asked him.

"I don't know, but I certainly risked missing breakfast."

"Oh, no," I whispered sarcastically. "Why aren't you there if you care so much?"

"I thought I'd walk you," he said, then held his hands

up. "Figure of speech. Walk with you. Companionship not chaperone."

"To breakfast?" I clarified.

He nodded. "Yep."

"I don't breakfast," I told him.

"You have to breakfast. It's the most important meal of the day."

I looked him over the best I was able to that early in the morning. "I don't *have* to do anything."

He would not be deterred. "No. But you really *should* breakfast."

I rolled my eyes. "You probably could have been finished by now if you hadn't wasted your time on me, Sasha."

His smile did have its charms. "No time on you is wasted, Elliott."

"Don't try and get cute with me."

"I'm honest to God not," he laughed. "I just legit did not think this was going to be a battle."

Alex, it appeared, was as stubborn as me. This was going one of two ways. Either we got into a massive and ridiculous fight about whether or not I went to breakfast and I got a few minutes before class to read my book. Or I could just take the high road and let him have this one, then rue my decision later.

I sighed. "All right. If I go with you to breakfast, will you leave me alone?"

For a moment, he looked hurt. But, quick as a wink, he was his unnecessarily chipper self and I thought I must have imagined anything else.

"Sure, yes. Scout's honour."

As we walked out the door, I asked, "Were you ever even in the Scouts?"

He laughed. "No. Heaven forbid. My mother would have had a fit if I suggested I wanted to join the Scouts."

I wasn't one to make a dig at other people's situations when I didn't know them all that well. Well, no. I was one. I'd just learnt to keep my mouth shut. Mostly.

"Did you…want to join the Scouts?" I asked hesitantly, not sure what else there was to say.

He shook his head as he waved to people we walked by. "Not really. Didn't even know they were a thing until I saw it in some movie or something. I had plenty of outside time to last me a lifetime growing up."

I nodded. "How nice for you."

He laughed. "If you say so."

We walked into the Dining Hall.

"Now, you'll probably need to know the lay of the land," he started.

"I think I'll be fine," I told him.

But, like previously, he wouldn't be deterred by mere protestations from me.

"Those are the wine kids," Alex said, pointing the one table. "The farming kids. The international kids, dividing themselves ever so subtly by country. The random riches – kids of lawyers, doctors, CEOS, and that. And last but not least, your people, the legacies."

"They're not my people," I informed him, a little more vehemently than intended.

He took the vehemence in stride. "Okay. Got it. Not your people."

"So, what are you?" I asked him in an effort to defrost the mood again.

"I'm a swimmer, thank you."

I rolled my eyes. "Yes. I knew that."

"Oh, stalking me already?" he teased.

My eyes rolled again. I indicated the dining hall. "From what bunch do you hail?"

He grinned. "I'm a wine kid."

I nodded. "Of course you are."

He shrugged. "Wine makes money."

"That it does," I said absently.

"What are you, then?" he asked.

I licked my lip as I turned back to him. "Hm?"

"If you don't belong to the legacies, from what…bunch do you hail?"

"Oh, none. Mum's a librarian."

"Cool."

I looked at him in case he wanted to rethink that statement.

"What?" he asked, totally innocently. "It is cool. Librarians are full of knowledge. They're like magic."

I tried to think about any remotely magical aspect of my mother and concluded that putting up with me would have to be it.

"I'm gonna…" I said, pointing to the breakfast line.

For another moment, I thought I saw that slight hurt to his face, but it was gone before I could be sure that's what

I saw. He smiled. "No worries. I gotta find the guys."

I gave him a nod. "I guess I'll see you later, then." It was going to be hard avoiding him when we were basically living together.

"That you will."

I watched him go and decided that the least I could do was find myself a hot beverage if I'd come all this way. Once procured, I found my usual empty table and pulled out my phone.

I opened my friends' chat, figuring it was about time to fill them in on the whole 'being bunked with a guy' debacle, but my fingers wouldn't type the words. As they hovered over the keypad, it just seemed trivial. Sure, Flick, Leah and Marsh would care that I was living with a guy, and an objectively attractive guy at that. But they'd also focus on the wrong thing. They wouldn't think about how annoying it was or he might be, they'd just lose their tiny little hormonal minds about how exciting it was.

Had I been some kind of normal person, then I might have done the same thing. For a second. The idea was what the stuff of rom-coms was made of – my guilty pleasures come true – but the reality was ever so slightly less…romantic. In every sense of the word.

Instead of giving them what was probably an important update on my life, I closed the chat and opened my book. One of my books. I always had at least one physical and one eBook on the go. I read for long enough that I ran out of tea and finally began hearing the familiar sounds of mass student movement.

I checked the clock on my phone and saw that it was definitely an appropriate time to be heading towards class. I saw Alex and his friends up ahead and decided to make a break for it before he felt the need to introduce me to whoever he might decide my people were.

It was a full day of lessons. Lessons worth the insane school fees. The day before had been a lot of introduction to classes and what our year was going to look like. Not Day Two. Day Two threw us in the deep end. Assignments were started; essays, practicals, research topics. I relished it.

Not only were there lessons, but administration to deal with. Namely ID card photo.

A corner of the entrance hall was set aside for students to get their new ID cards for the whole first week. As someone who didn't like having their picture taken, I'd put it off the day before. However, if Acacia was *anything* like my old school, then the majority of kids would be lining up on the last day, so today seemed preferable than kilometre-long lines. As it was, there was still a line, but it only took half of lunch.

"Here you go, Elliott," the ID card issuer said as they handed me the little plastic card that would be my ticket to most of the school. To their credit, they didn't bat an eye at my name. I guessed they must have seen them all in their time.

"Thanks," I told them, then did the obligatory move away while assessing the damage.

The damage that year was minimal. Yet again, totally unflattering, but the only person who was going to see it was the librarian and I liked to hope that they judged you more on the books you checked out than how photogenic you were.

I saw Alex throughout the day. Of course I did.

He was in our dorm during breaks to swap books over for the next lessons.

He was in the hallways, constantly surrounded by

people, those I recognised and those I didn't.

He was smiling. Always smiling. And laughing.

He also always said hi to me. Whether it was the actual words, a raised hand, or just a nod of his chin, he acknowledged my presence every time he saw me. I'd never been more annoyed at having my existence validated.

It was ridiculous, the way he annoyed me so much. It made no sense. My immediate appraisal was that he was a popular jock a-hole. The evidence would suggest a significant lack of the a-hole part. Maybe that was what annoyed me. No one in their right mind was *that* nice to someone they'd just met for no reason.

"Good day?" he asked as he walked into the dorm after school that day.

I looked up from my book, safely nestled in the window seat with a cup of tea. "Fine. You?" I felt obliged to return the goodwill.

He grinned as he nodded. "Great."

That much positivity was going to wear thin after a while.

He kicked his head towards me. "I see you've set up

camp."

"It has its tactical advantages. You didn't want to sit here?"

He looked me over like he had no idea where I'd come from or what language I spoke. "What? No. All good. You can have the...tactical advantage." He paused mid-step, then asked, "Are you expecting some sort of attack?"

It was an odd question, and one too quizzical to have been intended as witty repartee. It made me wonder if I was. My immediate answer would have been 'yes' had I not stopped to think about it. Just what kind of attack was I expecting?

"Always best to be prepared. Can't be snuck up on this way."

"Would it help if I loudly announced myself every time I entered the room?"

I smirked. "There's really no need. In fact, please don't feel you *have* to talk to me just because we're roommates." I thought I pulled off the earnest politeness more than the bitchy sarcasm.

"I don't feel like I *have* to talk to you. I want to talk to you."

My "Why?" I think fully conveyed that I was confused and baffled by anyone wanting to talk to me.

He shrugged. "You seem…cool."

I snorted. "Cool is something I'm not."

"Is that what you tell yourself to seem more aloof?" he asked.

That was a good shot. Real proper backhanded compliment. "Ouch. Okay. No. I just legitimately don't think I fall under the urban dictionary definition of 'cool'."

He laughed, "Who does?"

I looked him over pointedly. "Hello?"

"Naw, you think I'm cool?"

I rolled my eyes. "I think the rest of the school thinks so."

"They might think you are if you gave them a chance."

"Firstly, ew. No thank you. Secondly, if I have to talk to people, no."

"Of course not. We wouldn't want to run the risk of social interaction, now. Would we?"

I gave him a smile. "See? You get it."

He grinned. "You're one strange human, Elliott."

"Swamp witch," I corrected him.

He gave a little mock-bow. "My bad. In that case, you seem perfectly normal."

I inclined my head in the closest he was getting to a curtsey. "Thank you."

"Alex!" someone called as they literally slammed into our dorm door. "We've been waiting forever."

It was the red-head. Followed closely and nearly squashed against our door by the one with the light brown hair. They were both out of their uniforms

"Dude, what is taking you?"

Alex pointed in my direction. "We were sharing about our day."

"His was great," I told them.

They both nodded to me in greeting.

"Cool," red-head said. "But when you say ten minutes, you're usually ten minutes."

"I didn't want to be rude," Alex said as he started walking to his room, presumably to change for whatever they'd planned to do.

"Oh, no. Please," I said. "Feel free."

Alex smirked at me before turning to his friends and mock-whispering while pointing to me, "We're avoiding social interaction."

"Ohhhh," they both said, as though they had any idea what we were talking about.

Alex disappeared and I looked at the boys in the doorway. There was a very pregnant pause as we all sized each other up.

The red-head nodded. "Hey."

The other one nodded. "Hi."

I inclined my head. "Hi."

"How, er, are you settling in?" the other one asked.

I smiled politely. "Fine and dandy."

"Good." The red-head nodded again.

Another pause. I could have been more helpful. I could have asked questions of them or offered more information. But I enjoyed watching people squirm in those silences. I'd always liked them and it fascinated me that most other people didn't feel that way.

"You, ah, like reading, then?"

I held up the book in my hands. "It passes the time."

Another nod. "Cool."

"Everyone's got the third degree?" Alex asked as he re-emerged in jeans and a tee. Then, directed to me, said,

"Don't worry. I'll be back well before curfew. There'll be no drinking and no drugs."

I gave him a humoured look without breaking into a smile. "Good to know."

"Grampa here has to make sure he's in bed on time," the red-head chortled.

Alex wrapped an arm around his neck good-naturedly. "Why don't you do an early morning sport and see how late you can stay up, huh?" he laughed.

"See ya," the light brown haired one said as Alex and the red-head headed off down the hallway.

I gave him a small wave in response, pleased to have the space back to myself. I'd tried hanging out in my room the night before, but the window seat was way more comfortable. I wasn't about to claim ownership of the living room and be surly enough to make Alex feel like he couldn't hang around, but I was going to be glad when he didn't.

Chapter Five

I'd survived my first couple of weeks at boarding school. And, by survived, I mean I'd found something to entertain myself with. Namely, a 'Who could be most annoying' contest with Alex. I'm not sure that either of us started it on purpose, only that we both took great pleasure in it. One minute, it was just banter, the next we were pranking each other.

The first weekend saw very little of Alex. He was out with a girl on Friday – although, where kids dated at a boarding school was beyond me. He had an interschool swimming competition on the Saturday, followed by a party of sorts in the Recreation Room downstairs to celebrate his predictable win. Sunday was the first morning that he slept later than me. At least, he was in his room later than me. Who knew what he might have been getting up to in there?

Tuesday, I went to shower and found his budgie smugglers hanging, still wet, on the tap. I thought about using his toothbrush to remove them, but even I wasn't quite that evil. Instead, I used his shampoo bottle. I retaliated to his antic by leaving a pad on the counter. It backfired.

"Want me to scrounge some chocolate?" he asked casually, coming into the living room.

I looked up at him and frowned. "What?"

He pointed back to the bathroom. "I saw the pad out." He dropped his voice to a whisper. "Is it that time?"

"You're very blasé about it."

"Am I supposed to care?" He snorted. "You left it there on purpose. I was supposed to care."

I shrugged. "Most guys do."

"Most guys are morons. Most guys also probably didn't have an older sister who wished their younger brother was a sister."

"Aw, did you two play dress up?"

He smirked. "Sometimes. More to the point, she talked. A lot. We also shared a bathroom."

I sank further into the window seat, annoyed with my defeat. "Well, good on you having modern conceptions about women's health."

He shrugged. "Hey, it's not your fault your womb hates you."

I frowned at him.

"Not cool?" he asked. "My sister says it ALL the time."

I'd give him a pass on parroting for the sake of attempted bonding. "Well, she's not wrong."

"Poor little guy. Just wants to do his job."

"Yeah, and throws a hissy fit when it can't. Real peach."

"Does sound like a dick," Alex admitted.

We left it at that, and went our separate ways to concoct our prank plans. Well, I was concocting, so I assumed Alex was too.

Wednesday, I walked past his room with my head in a book. He appeared at his doorway and appeared to be saying something.

"What?" I asked, pulling my headphone out.

He visibly deflated and it was only then that I realised he had music playing loudly.

I smiled. "Was that meant to bother me?"

He sighed. "It was meant to."

I waved my headphone at him. "Sorry."

On Thursday, every cupboard opened up to inanimate objects with googly eyes stuck on them. My toothbrush. The milk in the bar fridge. Even my tea cup. It was a fair effort. It tended to freak me out rather than annoy me, but I had to admire his chutzpah.

He walked into the bathroom while I was brushing my teeth – to be fair, I'd left the door open – and I held my toothbrush out to him.

"I like what you did here."

He grinned. "Yeah?"

I nodded. "Not scary at all."

He snorted. "You're scared of googly eyes?"

I spat into the sink. "Apparently, yes. Turns out, I like my inanimate objects to stay inanimate."

He leant towards me and mock-whispered, "You know the eyes don't bring them to life?"

I brandished my toothbrush just in front of his face.

"Tell that to my fight or flight mode every time I open a cupboard."

He laughed and we said our goodnights.

Friday night, a different girl to the week before knocked on the dorm door and introduced herself as "Lara, looking for Alex? We've got a date."

I didn't need all the information, but I could work with it to annoy Alex. "So good of him to go out tonight. You know, after everything," I said in an exaggerated whisper.

Her brows furrowed in confusion. "What do you mean?"

"Oh," I feigned surprise. "He didn't tell you?"

She shook her head. "Tell me what?" She leant towards me like we were sharing a deliciously gossipy secret.

I looked around the room. "He had a little accident at practice today. Down there…" I whispered.

Her eyes went wide. "Is he okay?"

I nodded. "He will be. But he's out of commission for a while. Not that he wants to talk about it. You understand."

She nodded quickly. "No. No. Of course not. Poor Alex."

I nodded as well. "Poor Alex indeed. Don't mention it, but I'm sure he'd appreciate it if you…steered clear. If you get my drift."

Now her eyes went wide with understanding. "Yes. Sure. Of course. Thanks for telling me."

I shrugged as though it was honestly through the goodness of my own heart. "Don't mention it." I paused. "But really, don't mention it. He's very sensitive about it."

"Oh, Lara. Hey. You're here," Alex said as he came out of his room.

I quickly put my finger to my lips before he looked my way.

"You didn't want to tell me she was here?" he asked, his lips tipped in a crooked smile.

"She just got here," I told him.

He looked between us like he was looking for jokes, but couldn't see any. "Cool. Well, I'll see you later, E."

I nodded. "Later."

He and Lara left, and I was still reading in the window seat when he got back from his date a few hours later, but well within curfew.

"That was quick," I noted.

"Yeah," he said absently. "Weird, though."

"Oh, why?" I asked innocently.

He looked at me like he was just realising I was there. "Oh. Uh. No. Nothing. Probably. She just…" He shrugged. "Just didn't seem into it."

I snorted despite my best efforts. "Oh?" I still tried playing innocent.

His gaze sharpened on me. "What do you know?"

I shrugged. "Nothing."

A smile tugged at the corner of his lips despite himself. "What did you do?"

I shrugged again, looking around coyly. "I definitely didn't tell her you had an accident at practice and might have been…" I pointed down, "out of commission for a while."

He looked torn between impressed and annoyed. I couldn't for the life of me work out what emotion was going to win.

"That was…" he started, his tongue running along his teeth. "That was a good one. Yep. Okay. Fine." He gave a single nod. "Good night, Elliott."

"Good night, Sasha," I said as he strode purposefully to

his room.

His expression was relatively neutral but, even after only a couple of weeks, I knew him well enough to know retaliation was coming.

The next day, he sent me a barrage of text messages updating me about his life constantly. Starting with a very early breakfast. It was like a 'day in the life of' picture book downloading directly to my Acacia App. It didn't help that he had another swim meet, so there was a lot random, half-naked body parts.

When he sauntered in that night, he gave me the biggest smile like we'd been exchanging pleasantries all day.

"Cute," I told him.

He batted his eyelids. "Thank you."

"That was the most action I've seen in some time."

His smile turned wry. "Oh, my."

I tried not to laugh. "My phone. I meant my phone." I kicked my head to the side. "Although, also true of any other meaning."

He nodded. "Good to know."

Monday was delivery day. The day we got our 'essentials' delivered; toiletries, tea bags, sanitary products. Things we might have run out of and couldn't be trusted to go to the closest shops to get for ourselves. I was the first one back in the dorm after drop off, so I took a quick peek at Alex's and replaced his deodorant with mine.

His response? "Thanks, E. Now I smell like flowers." Complete with cheeky wink.

I had to admit, I really liked the smell of his. Then I realised it reminded me of him and put it at the back of my bottom-most drawer to never speak of it again.

Tuesday, he'd duct taped an air horn under my desk chair which scared the living daylights out of me when I went to do my homework. I could hear him cackling from his room.

Wednesday, I overheard him talking to one of his friends about yet another girl he was going to see that weekend and the impression he was a bit of a womaniser solidified. So, while he was out, I left him a message on the kitchenette saying 'Alex, we need to talk ASAP' and left the signature completely illegible. I then watched as he scrambled to work out who'd left it for him until I broke down in laughter and he guessed it was me. That one also semi-backfired because he then insisted we talk quoting, "the note said so, Elliott".

Thursday, I walked out of my bedroom to a shower of popcorn Alex had rigged above my door. He was waiting in the living room and hooted with laughter when he saw me.

"That was an epic waste of popcorn," I informed him.

He toppled over the back of the couch with laughter and I heard, "Worth it!"

As his face popped up again, I pulled a piece of popcorn out of my curls and ate it before sticking my tongue out at him. That only served to send him into hoots again.

On Friday, he had his friends over to our dorm and they were all on their loudest behaviour.

"Yo, dudes," Alex said as I walked into the room. "You remember *Elliott*?" He smirked at me.

"It's Lottie right?" Birdman asked, elbowing Alex companionably.

"Yes. Lottie," I answered him, throwing a smirk of my own in Alex's direction.

Alex looked bummed that his friends had sided with me instead of him.

"I don't think we've been formally introduced," the

short red-head said, in yet another stripey t-shirt. "I'm Zac. Parker." He paused, then said quickly, "Zac Parker."

I nodded. "Pleasure." *Sort of.*

Then came the big blond Viking. "Luke Cook."

"He's that big 'cos he's a rugby boy," Alex said through a mouthful of food.

"Makes sense," I said. *Did it?* "Hi."

The lean one with the light brown hair he had to flick out of his face. "Sam Cox."

"Nice to meet you." *Was it?*

"Friends call him Fret," Zac said.

I looked between them. "Fret?"

And the tall, lanky one with the dark blond hair known as Birdman. "There's a whole story. Was hilarious. Probably had to be there. Henry Bird."

"Ah. Hence Birdman," I observed.

"Indeed."

I nodded again. "Good to know." *It was.*

"We weren't being *too loud* for you to study, were we, E?" Alex asked.

I shook my head. "No. Fine. My mum throws *much* louder parties."

73

"You two still having a pissing contest?" Luke the Rugby Viking asked.

"Excuse me?" I asked.

Zac of the red hair nodded and pointed between us. "The whole 'who's more annoying than who' contest."

I looked at Alex as though he'd betrayed a secret. "Well, I think we know who won."

Alex nodded. "Me."

"No!" I said. "It was totally me. I didn't have any ruined dates because of fake crotch injuries. Did I?"

Fret actually spat his drink out with laughter. "She what?"

"Oh, she so won," Birdman said.

"What?" Alex was highly indignant. "She did not!"

"*That's* what Lara meant," Zac said slowly, like pieces were falling into place.

"What did Lara mean when?" Alex asked.

Zac nodded. "Yeah. Last week, she asked me if you were okay. She said she knew she wasn't meant to know, but she felt bad for you." He snorted. "The actual reason is so much better than anything I came up with."

Alex looked at me in something not as strong as a glare,

but was definitely annoyance. "Fine," he muttered as he sank into the couch. "She won."

"You want to join us for some games, Lottie?" Birdman asked with a smile.

I shook my head. "Thanks, boys. I've got homework."

"But it's Friday night!" Fret said.

I nodded. "It is. But if I don't do my homework now, what excuse will I have to not hang out with you?" I gave him a grin so he'd know I didn't mean it totally personally.

"Even swamp witches can't avoid social interaction forever, E!" Alex called as I headed back into my room.

"Just watch me!" I called back before closing the door.

Chapter Six

Life went on. I continued to survive at Acacia Academy with Alex Landry for a roommate. Our prank war, by some unspoken agreement, was under a ceasefire order. That's not to say we didn't try to annoy each other, but we didn't go to quite such extraordinary lengths, leaving it more to sassy banter and witty remarks.

Alex continued getting up before the sun and going to bed just when my brain started to feel properly awake. It was like living with Mum, so a nice reminder of home.

Mum and I exchanged texts on a regular basis. Nothing of import, just generic 'this happened' and 'that happened' and 'love you, miss you' messages. The same as we'd usually send each other, just more often now. Neither

Mum nor I were really phone people, so we felt no inclination to actually speak to each other.

I spent my meals at the end of my table in the Dining Hall, my nose in a book. I spent breaks either in the dorm or library, perfecting my resting bitch face so no one talked to me. It worked. For the most part. Alex refused to be deterred by any face I gave him, and his friends followed suit.

It wasn't just them, though. One lunch time, I was approached by a bunch of girls with perfect manicures and not a hair out of place. They looked me over like they didn't find me particularly impressive or interesting. I'm pleased to report the feeling was mutual.

"You're Alex Landry's roommate, yeah?" one of them asked.

I looked over my book at them. "I'm Lottie," I answered.

"Lottie, like as in Elliott?" she asked.

I sighed and put my book down. "Lottie as in Elliott," I clarified, feeling like it'd be nice to be known as me for once rather than my relation to my roommate or my father.

"What kind of name is Elliott?" another asked.

"The one my parents gave me," I told her.

The first one flicked her hand at the second one who'd spoken. I recognised a shushing motion when I saw one. "I hear you're a legacy."

I frowned. "Who did you hear that from?"

"Is it true?"

I looked around as though I thought someone was going to come and save me. "My dad was an Acacia alumnus," I said carefully.

Suddenly, she smiled. "I'm Liz Spencer." As if they were an after-thought, she pointed to the girls with her. "Annabelle. Victoria. Lauren."

I nodded. "Lovely." It wasn't.

There was a pause and I didn't know if I was supposed to be offering her more information or whether I was supposed to recognise something about her name. It sounded familiar, but I doubted it was because I'd heard of her parents.

"I'm Vice President of the Legacy Society Committee," Liz said finally.

I nodded. "Good for you."

"The Year Eleven chapter of the Society meets on

Wednesdays after school in the Wattle House Rec Room."

We looked at each other without saying anything more for a few moments. I looked to the three girls behind her as though they might know what Liz was waiting for. Eventually, it hit me.

"Oh!" I cried, unable to help smiling. "Oh, you think I'll… Oh, no. Thanks, but no. It's not for me."

Liz frowned. "Not for you?" she asked, clearly wondering at the audacity of me.

"Thanks for thinking of me, but I won't be there."

"But you're a legacy."

"Isn't half this school legacies?" I asked, waving around a nonchalant hand.

Liz's nostrils flared. And I mean *flared*. "Forty-seven percent."

I nodded. "There you go. So, you'll hardly miss me."

"But you're Elliot Hopkins' daughter."

I nodded again. "I'm also Elliott Hopkins in my own right. My dad might have cared for all this legacy crap – my grandparents certainly do – but I don't. It's not you, it's me."

I could have sworn smoke was about to billow out of

Liz's nose or ears, maybe both. Maybe her arse. Either way, she looked none too pleased with me as a person.

"Fine," she said. "It's not like it's compulsory. You'll just be the only legacy in the whole school not involved with your chapter, but whatever."

I think she thought I'd care more than I did. "That's fine. Probably for the best. You'll all have a better time without me."

Liz flicked her hair over her shoulder, gave me the stink-eye to put all previous stink-eyes to shame, then all four of them turned on their heels and sashayed away.

I thought very little of it until I saw Alex later.

"I hear you defied Liz Spencer," he chuckled as we passed each other in the hallway.

"Is that going to get me in a load of trouble?" I asked him, not actually concerned at all about what Liz Spencer might have thought of me.

He flailed his arms in an exaggerated shrug. "Time will tell."

He managed to say it in such a way that I suddenly worried about what was coming. For the first time in my life, I second-guessed my mouth's take-charge attitude.

Would it have been better just to go to the damn meetings?

Alex laughed, "I'm sure you'll be fine."

I wasn't entirely reassured, but I decided to not let it get to me. I might have told Mum I was going to join a club or group or something, but that didn't have to be some kind of Legacy Society where I was probably going to have to endure some kind of weird initiation rituals.

No.

It'd be fine.

Liz Spencer would forget about me by the end of the day when some new excitement came along.

Whether she forgot about me or not, I suffered no repercussions and got though the rest of my day safely. I was in my room studying when I heard the boys arrive to hang out with Alex. They weren't quite on their loudest behaviour, but they didn't sound like they were trying to keep it down either.

I ignored them for the most part. Their conversations revolved around sport or girls or homework; boring standard stuff. That was until my name came up.

"You know, for a self-professed swamp witch, she looks good," I heard Birdman say.

"She's hot," Zac agreed. "Alex, don't you reckon she's hot?"

"She's all right," Alex answered.

"Distance-wise, she's extremely tappable," Zac said.

"Looks-wise, she is also extremely tappable," Birdman added.

"You haven't thought about it even once?" Fret asked.

Alex laughed. "She's not my type."

"Okay," Luke said. "Pretend she wasn't a kick-arse devil may care young woman who doesn't have a very attractive 'come bite me' personality–"

"That sounds pretty good to me," Birdman commented.

"Pretend," Luke continued, "she's not awesome, what about then?"

Alex laughed again. "Sure. If she wasn't awesome, she'd be tappable."

"Shame I'm so awesome, then," I joked, leaning in my bedroom doorway.

They all turned to look at me with expressions ranging from 'crap' to 'lols'. Birdman, Fret and Alex were changed into casual clothes and Luke and Zac were still in their uniforms. Pretty standard Acacia protocol for post-lesson time during the week, I was discovering.

"Bold of you to say all that where I can hear it," I commented dryly.

Alex shrugged, alarmingly casual. "It's hard to have secrets in such a close living space."

The way he said it was just a touch foreboding. Like he was going to slowly peel my secrets away from me layer by layer until no two people in the universe knew each other better. Which I knew, as soon as I thought it, was ridiculous.

"True," Zac noted as I started getting myself a cup of tea. "Like I know my roommate likes Rule 34 porn."

I felt my nose wrinkle. "How do you know that? What is that?"

"Ha!" Alex crowed. "Something you don't know."

"Wait," I said. "Is that the one where 'if it exists, there's porn of it'?"

Alex deflated. "You do know it."

Zac nodded. "That's the one."

"Is nothing sacred anymore?" I asked.

"Why?" Alex smirked. "You worried I'll find out what kind of porn you like?"

I picked up my cup of tea and smirked back at him. "I have no shame, Sasha," I said as I went back into my room.

I heard them talking about what kind of porn they thought I'd like, but it quickly shifted back to sports. I managed to tune them out for the most part and lost track of time.

At some point, Alex knocked on my open door. "You coming to dinner?"

I was learning it was just easier to lean into their niceness. It saved me a whole lot of extra talking. "Sure." I hit save on my file and closed my laptop lid.

"I'm *so* hungry," Zac was saying as we walked back out to the living room.

"I'm so hungrier," Fret said, rubbing his stomach.

Zac shook his head. "I'm so hungry, I'm getting everything."

"Nuh-uh. I'm getting everything."

"Children," I laughed. "I'm sure there's enough everything for everyone."

The six of us started walking towards the Dining Hall. Zac and Fret were ahead, still arguing about who was hungrier. Luke wandered along behind them all strong and silent like. I somehow ended up at the back between Birdman and Alex.

"Luke'll eat twice as much as both of them," Birdman said to me quietly.

"Cook's twice the size of both of them," Alex chuckled.

"Yeah," Birdman mused. "Unless there's pizza."

Alex clicked his fingers at him over me. "True. Zac's been known to eat his weight in pizza," he told me.

"His actual weight?" I asked.

Birdman snorted. "No."

"His figurative weight," Alex explained.

"And how much is that?"

Alex shrugged. "More than Cook anyway."

"That's hardly fair. You know how Luke gets when he has too much gluten."

Alex chuckled. "Dude's on the loo for hours!"

I smiled despite myself. "I figured that one out. Thanks, though."

"You're smarter than you look," Alex quipped.

"Which is impressive," Birdman added.

Alex nodded. "Because you look freaking smart."

"Thank you?" I wasn't sure if that was a compliment or

not.

"Pizza!" we heard from up ahead.

I looked over and saw Zac with his hands in the air.

"Poor Luke," I commented.

Alex and Birdman laughed.

We all lined up together and got our dinners. It wasn't really poor Luke. There were multiple options for mains. I can't say I was surprised when I saw Zac headed for their table with his tray piled up with pizza slices.

Alex was behind me so, after I got my dinner, I smiled at him and said, "I'll see you later."

"Still not sitting with us?" he asked, a rueful smile at his lips.

"My book won't finish itself."

He nodded. "All right then."

"See ya later, Lottie," Birdman said.

I gave him a nod and headed for my empty spot.

It was difficult not to notice Zac's overconsumption of pizza, nor Fret's attempt to keep up with him. They both pretty much needed rolling back to their dorms. I want to say I dawdled over my food because I got lost in my book, but I'd be lying. I just wanted to see how their competition went.

Later that night, I came out of my room to find Alex in nothing but a towel, once again.

"Do you not own clothes?" I asked facetiously, clearly knowing he did own clothes.

He smirked. "I thought you'd gone to bed."

"Unlike you, Grampa, I'll be up for a few more hours yet."

"I've said it once and I'll say it again, you try…" He turned and something got dislodged as his towel tried making a break for it.

"Dude!" I cried as I averted my eyes and closed them for good measure.

But I'd not averted and he'd not salvaged the towel quick enough. The momentary flash of full-frontal had apparently been burned into my retinas.

He laughed. "My bad."

"When I said I'd see you later…" I muttered, hand still firmly planted to my eyes.

"I *am* decent."

I moved one finger to peek out of and saw he hand a firm hand on covering everything.

"I'm not sure that word could ever apply to you."

He snorted. "It *was* an accident."

"I'm so glad you didn't flash me on purpose! Talk about not being able to keep secrets in close quarters…"

"Hey, that's hardly fair. It's just been me baring secrets here. You haven't bared anything."

I looked him over. "And I don't plan to."

He looked at a loss for words to say. Or maybe he'd come up with too many quips and couldn't decide which one to use. So he just smiled at me, a deep warmth in his eyes. I couldn't stop myself smiling back.

"I'm not going to bed, but I am definitely going to hide in my room now," I informed him with a firm nod.

His grin widened. "Okay, then."

"Maybe you can invest in some clothes."

More widening. "I'll try to remember to take a change of clothes to the bathroom with me."

"You could always just go straight to your room?"

He nodded as he ran a hand over his chin. "Now, there's an idea."

My eyes dropped involuntarily to his crotch. "I'll leave you to it."

Humour played all across his face. "Okay, then."

"Good night, Alex."

"Good night, Lottie."

Chapter Seven

Alex, thankfully, stopped wandering around our living room in nothing but a towel. I wanted to say he was just being gentlemanly, but I suspected he also was a little embarrassed about the towel slip.

"'Sup, Lottie," Luke said with a smile as he walked by me in the hallway before recess and I nodded back in greeting.

It was like that. Everywhere I went, whenever I saw them, they said hello. I was slowly getting used to my existence being so frequently acknowledged.

I grabbed a muffin and dropped into my usual seat. Alone as usual. I watched the other students laughing and chatting with their friends. It made me think of my friends back home. My friends who, even for me, I hadn't talked to properly in a while. I'd thought about them a lot, but I'd never been good at small talk with anyone other than Mum.

I pulled up the chat thread for Flick, Leah and Marsh. Nothing. Nothing that pertained to me anyway. I looked back over the last few messages and realised that, over the last few weeks, we'd just been messaging less and less until it was all just shared posts one of us found amusing. I wondered if they had another thread going without me, or whether they'd just stopped using messages so much.

Part of me felt a bit saddened by it, like I'd lost something good. Another part of me realised that I'd been surviving without it quite well. The benefit to being an introverted bookworm was that, as much as I cared about certain people, I could do without their physical – or, in this case, online – presence quite well.

It was putting into stark contrast why I constantly ate alone, why I sat by myself in classes, and why I walked the halls without a posse of people to laugh at my very witty jokes. On one hand, I cared. On the other, I didn't care enough to be bothered doing anything about it.

After Recess, as I was walking to class, I almost ran into Liz Spencer and her friends. As we did the 'who's going which way' dance, I gave Liz an apologetic smile. The smile she returned was very definitely not friendly. But she said nothing. She clearly didn't like me, but she and her friends just got around me and went on their way.

"Lottie!" Fret and Zac cried when I passed them in the hallway later that day.

As I had with Luke earlier, I nodded back in greeting.

"How you going?" Zac asked.

I gave them another nod. "Same old, same old."

"You coming to the swim meet on Saturday?" Fret asked.

I frowned. "Why would I go to the swim meet? Besides, don't you have your own sports to go to?"

"Soccer's terms two and three," Fret said.

"And baseball's Sundays," Zac said.

Something hit me. "Who do you even play out here?"

Zac grinned. "Local schools and teams mainly. Sometimes we do weekend tournaments with schools further away."

I shook my head. "All in the name of 'excellence',

huh?"

Fret nodded. "Yup."

As though by unspoken decision, we went our own ways. Me to class, them to whatever they had on then. As I walked to my usual seat in class, Birdman smiled at me and I, once again, nodded back in greeting.

Why they all felt the need to say hello to me was beyond me. It was clear from the interactions they had with the larger student body that they were popular kids. They had kids giggling over them, others fawning, and still others hanging on their every word. People liked them. What for, I was yet to see. But maybe, just maybe it had something to do with the fact they looked like stuck up wankers but didn't act like it. Were they arrogant? Was life easy for them? Did they seem to get whatever they wanted? Yes. But I also didn't see them torment anyone, speak down to anyone, or shove anyone in a locker.

Something had to be wrong with them, though.

Since when were popular kids ever nice?

But then, for the most part, most of the kids at Acacia Academy seemed nice. Enough. Which wasn't to say there wasn't teasing or rumours or bullying to some degree. It was a couple of buildings full to bursting with teenagers after all, but it wasn't overt, the whole school didn't know about it, and there wasn't any kind of West Side Story faction bollocks going on.

Bad words about someone were whispered among groups and rumours were incredibly vague and more often about the exploits of past students than current students.

Teasing seemed to be more a one-off play to the moment with some expert timing sort of thing, rather than on-going agony.

Bullying, I hadn't seen much of. There wasn't like the kid who started fights with everyone. There was no bad boy who hustled kids for their lunch money, or equivalent. No one was pushed in the corridors. Cliques weren't battling it out for supremacy. No one was crying in the toilets on a daily basis. The worst we had were people like Liz Spencer who thought she was better than everyone else; you could just see it on her face.

The place was... It was disturbingly realistic and boringly normal.

It was a typical Australian high school filled with typical Australian teenagers.

Or maybe, as the new kid, I just didn't see a lot of the nuances.

Whichever it was, there wasn't much to complain about. Which was unfortunate because I enjoyed complaining.

Chapter Eight

On Wednesday morning of Week 6, Alex wasn't bugging me about being late for breakfast. Instead, he was wheeling a small suitcase out of his room.

I looked him over. "Where are you going?"

"City."

"What for?"

"Swimming carnival."

"When is it?"

"Tonight."

"And you're only going now?"

He nodded. "They try to restrict the number of days we miss for carnivals."

"Seems like an awful lot of trouble."

"Yeah, well that's what happens when you're an Acacia Angelshark." The 'hoorah' harrumph was left unsaid, but I still heard it.

"Will your parents be there at least?"

"Unlikely. Eh. Maybe. I'm not going to hold my breath."

"Wouldn't it be easier to go to a school closer to the carnivals?"

"It would."

"But your parents sent you here?"

"They were going to send me to the city to board, but why not be exceptional?" The question was clearly rhetoric, completed as it was by jazz-hands.

"So, you just have to travel to the city every few weeks instead?"

He nodded. "All five hours there and back. Usually on the day of comps."

"That sucks."

He flashed me a smile. "But it is. No use worrying over things I can't change."

That seemed like a dangerously healthy outlook on life. I wanted no part of it.

97

"You'll be back tonight then?" I asked.

"Why?" he teased. "You gonna miss me?"

I might have maybe missed someone being close by, which made me realise that I appreciated his existence and proximity, but I wasn't about to tell him that. "No. Just wondering if it'll be safe to wander around naked or not."

He snorted. "It'll be safe. Comp finishes at half nine, so we're staying over."

"Oh, night in a big town. Mind you don't get lost."

Alex laughed. "We can go together someday and you can show me around proper."

I looked down at my book. "I might just do that."

"Don't do anything I wouldn't do." I heard the smile in his voice. "I'll see you tomorrow."

I nodded. "See you tomorrow. Good luck!" I called quickly as he headed out.

His hand raised in a wave as he disappeared into the corridor.

With Alex gone, I'd thought my day would be different.

Without Alex, why would the other boys have bothered saying hello to me? Why would they feel obliged to wave or smile or talk to me?

98

I certainly doubted it was my sunny disposition.

And yet, they did.

Clearly the reason they talked to me wasn't *just* because I was Alex's roommate and they were polite young men.

When I registered someone close to my spot in the Dining Hall at lunch, I assumed it was one of the guys again. It wasn't.

"Hey," came an unknown voice and I looked up.

Standing over me was a guy. A guy I didn't know. Which wasn't hard. I basically knew five people in the whole school and actively shied away from connecting with anyone else.

He was kinda cute. Non-descript in his green and grey Acacia uniform. His hair was almost black and, standing up, I bet he wouldn't be much taller than me. He was smiling, his brown eyes shining brightly in welcome.

"Hey…" I said slowly, unable to help wondering if this was some sort of trick or, at the very least, going to involve unwanted social interaction.

"I'm Jake," he said with a nod.

"Lottie…" I said, still slowly, looking around surreptitiously like I was trying to work out who he belonged to and if they were going to come and collect him, lost puppy that he was.

"Nice to meet you."

I nodded. "Same." When he didn't say anything more, I had to speak. "Did you... Can I help you with something?"

He shook his head. "I've seen you around and just wanted to introduce myself."

I felt myself smile, although I didn't really know why. "Oh, okay then. Hi."

His smile was kinda nice. "Hi."

I wasn't quite so closed off from the world to not realise the guy was flirting with me. I just wasn't sure why I might be flirting back. Because I was. I tucked my hair behind my ear, my tell for when I was getting a little flirty.

"So..." Jake started slowly.

"So?"

"Can I message you sometime?"

I was smiling like the five-year-old who's just been set loose in Blackebys on her birthday. I didn't know what was wrong with me.

I nodded to Jake. "Sure. You can find me under room

605. Elliott Hopkins."

Jake's easy charm stuttered for a moment with surprise, but he kept hold of it. "You're Alex Landry's roommate?"

I let go a deep breath. "I tend to think of myself as Lottie, but that also works."

He gave me a lop-sided grin. "I didn't mean… Just, your name's done the rounds. Landry and his mates think it's hilarious he got landed with a girl."

"Oh, I'm aware. The humour isn't lost on me either, I just don't feel the need to broadcast it to the world."

"It's hardly the world. Someone asked Cook about it in the locker room."

Cook was Luke who played… Rugby Viking!

"You play rugby, too?"

He nodded. "Yep."

"Jakey!" someone called and he turned for a second.

"I better go. I'll message you…Lottie."

I nodded. "Sounds good…Jake."

He gave me another smile, then disappeared.

Curious as to who this Jake was, I opened my Acacia App to do a search. Looking up Jakes was unhelpful. I knew this because it was at this point that I realised that it wasn't just the librarians who'd see my ID photo. Everyone on the Acacia App had their ID photo as their profile picture. And I couldn't rightly tell if any of the Jakes I found were the Jake who'd spoken to me.

I was just going to have to wait and see if he messaged me.

On Saturday night, Alex came out to the living room, pausing at the mirror to pull his hair up.

"I'm going to the rec room," he said. "Wanna come?"

I shook my head. "I have a date."

He whirled around and I couldn't read the look on his face. "What?"

I laughed and held up my book. "With my book. Jesus. What did you think I meant?"

He started to shake his head, then switched to nodding. "No. Nothing. I knew what you meant."

"Have a good night, then," I said to him.

He looked at me once more, then nodded. "You, too."

And I planned to. Unlimited tea and books in the snuggly window seat. My idea of a good night in.

It wasn't all that long, however, until Alex wandered back in, followed by the boys.

"I thought you were going to the rec room?" I accused him.

He nodded. "I did go to the rec room. That's where I found these guys."

"Hey, Lottie," Birdman said.

"'Sup?" Nodded Fret.

I inclined my head. "I *was* reading in peace. I'll take it to my room and leave you boys to it."

A resounding, 'No,' chorused from the five of them in varying combinations as they all talked over each other.

I couldn't help but smile. "It's fine. I don't want to get in the way."

"You won't be in the way," Luke said.

"Nah, hang out with us," Alex agreed.

I looked them over. "Forfeit a night of reading to hang out with you lot?"

Alex's grin was infectious. "Why not? I'd feel bad

103

kicking you into your room."

I shrugged. "I guess I can stay. I can't promise I'll pay attention."

Alex nodded. "I'll take it."

I curled myself up in the arm chair while Alex pulled a bag of popcorn and a bag of party mix out of the cupboard.

"Okay," he said as he chucked the bags to Birdman and Zac. "Do we introduce Lottie to Mario Kart Deluxe or the Fast franchise."

I snorted from behind my book.

"What?" Alex asked. "You too cool for car racing?"

"Hardly. I like how you assume I'm ignorant of both those things. I also like how you're keeping male stereotypes alive and well."

"What can I say?" Zac said. "Cars are awesome."

I nodded. "They are."

"Why is she so cool?" Zac asked the room at large.

Birdman smiled at me. "She is awesome."

"Why do you hide yourself away?" Fret lamented.

"I'm not hiding," I told them. "I just don't throw myself at any old person who comes along."

"You either think very little of us, or you," Luke noted.

"*Porque no los dos*," Alex suggested.

"Did you have to say that," I laughed. "Seriously. All I want is tacos."

"Every time, right?" Zac said, pointing at me.

I nodded. "Yes. Every time."

The ad had become part of pop culture. I'd never seen it air, but I'd seen it on YouTube.

"Well, we're shit outta luck on tacos," Alex said.

"Why do you think we never get tacos for dinner?" Fret asked.

Alex shrugged. "Probably too fiddly."

"I'd have thought pizza was too fiddly," Birdman said.

"Shh!" Zac hissed harshly. "Don't jinx it!"

"You haven't had enough pizza to sort you for a lifetime?" I asked.

Zac shook his head. "Never. Pizza is life."

I nodded. "Fair enough."

"You know," Fret said. "Having a girl," he left an ample pause, "friend has its advantages."

"Yeah?" I asked. "What is that exactly?"

"Well, we've got like a direct line into the female psyche."

"You went with Psychology this year, eh, mate?" Alex asked him.

"I did." Fret seemed quite pleased with himself. "But my point stands. Lottie here can help us understand the ways of the female heart."

"And exactly what female heart are you interested in?" Birdman asked him.

Fret shrugged. "None. Yet. But Lottie can make them all less scary."

I couldn't keep my amusement in anymore. I busted out into laughter.

"What?" Fret asked.

I shook my head. "No. I mean. The theory is sound."

"But?"

"But you're forgetting one very important detail."

"Which is?" Birdman asked.

"Which is I have no idea how other humans operate."

"But you're a girl."

I nodded. "I am."

"So, you at least know what girls don't like."

I shrugged. "I know what I don't like."

Alex leant towards me. "Tell me more about–" he

started.

But Birdman interrupted. "Well, surely whatever you don't like will cover everything someone else might not like."

I smiled at him. "Is that some kind of commentary on my personality, Henry?"

He grinned. "Just an observation."

"Oh, yeah? Of what?" I wondered if he'd actually say it.

"Of the fact you seem to dislike a lot of stuff. So, everything you dislike… Probably covers the spectrum of stuff anyone else might not like."

"So, I'm like the repository of what girls won't like?"

Birdman shrugged with a wry smile. "If the shoe fits."

I couldn't help but find the positive spin on an otherwise negative personality trait both amusing and somewhat flattering.

I hung out with the boys, playing games on the console and chatting and eating junk, until about ten when, as one, the four of them started stretching and standing up.

"Has this got to do with Alex's absurd bedtime?" I asked.

Birdman smirked. "Grampa needs his beauty sleep."

"Hey," Alex said. "I wasn't born this good looking, you know."

He and Birdman exchanged a joking smile.

"Yeah, I know," Birdman said, nodding.

"Oh, you know?" Alex asked and Birdman nodded again. "Yeah. I'll give you good looking."

The two of them scuffled around the room while the others said good night.

I almost told them they could stay because I'd be up for another couple of hours at least. But something held me back. Whether it was my introvert tendencies, a worry that they wouldn't want to hang out with just me, or something else, I didn't know.

Finally, they were all gone, Alex was in bed and I was sitting in the window seat, looking out over the moonlit grounds of Acacia.

Weirdly, I hadn't felt like the odd man out. I felt like I'd found a place I could – maybe, if I bothered – belong. Alex's friends were easy to get along with. They didn't care if I came across as what other people warned me could sound acerbic. They didn't mind that I said whatever came into my head. They didn't care I didn't mind my manners quite as well as I could have. They didn't care I professed my preference for solitude.

They just legitimately seemed to like me for me.

Chapter Nine

I'd almost forgotten about meeting Jake and his promise to message me. That was until I received an Acacia App notification of a new message from one Jacob Harman.

Jacob Harman

Hey Lottie, I found you! How's things?

Jake.

Before I replied, I clicked on his profile and saw he was in the year ahead of us, a member of the First Thirteen of the rugby team, and a prefect. On paper, the guy looked good. In real life, the guy looked pretty good, too. What was the harm in seeing where things were going to go?

Elliott Hopkins

You did! My things are fine. How are

I wasn't expecting a reply straight away, but I did sit staring at my screen for a while just in case.

"Are you trying to read two books at once?" Alex asked from his place on the couch.

"Why do you say that?" I asked from the window seat.

"Just, you were staring at a paperback and now you're staring at your phone, which I assume is an eBook." He was focussing on his game so I had no idea how he knew what I was up to.

Not wanting to admit I was messaging a boy for some reason, I just said, "It doesn't hurt to try."

Alex smirked. "Of course it doesn't. You nerd."

No one but my mum had ever called me a nerd with such – dare I say it – fondness. Like it was a good thing. Even Flick, Leah and Marsh had always said it with a bit of a sour tinge to it. As though they accepted it, but wished I wasn't quite so much.

I was distracted from my wondering thoughts by my phone buzzing.

Another Acacia App message notification.

Jacob Harman

Things are good. What are you up to this
weekend?

Elliott Hopkins

Just being. You?

Jacob Harman

Same. Although got our first pre-season
practice tomorrow. Not looking forward
to that!

I wasn't quite sure what to say to that. As I already
established, I was bad at small-talk. It made some sense to
me that the top teams would start practice before the
season actually started. Maybe it was all the fiction I
consumed, but that seemed to be a thing people did when
they thought they were quite good at what they did.

First Thirteen sounded weird to me, though. Why did
they call the top team the 'First...'? I mean I guess it was
because they were the Firsts team. My cousin's school just
called those the 'A' teams.

"Do you know what?" Alex mused suddenly.

"What?" I replied, still wondering what I should reply
to Jake.

112

"I should have played cricket."

"Yeah? Why is that?" was a weird question for me to ask because I didn't often care about other people's motivations or random thoughts.

Alex dropped the console controller into his lap and stared ahead. "Being in the First Eleven sounds way cooler than being on the swim team."

It was like he could read my mind or something.

"I guess. But are you any good at cricket?"

He looked at me with a smirk. "Terrible. Worse than terrible. Abysmal."

"I'm impressed you know such a big word."

"Terrible's not that big a word," he teased and I couldn't help smiling at him.

"Then you wouldn't have made it to the First Eleven, would you? What's better? Trying and constantly failing to get on the First Eleven or being the *god* of the swim team?"

He chuckled as he restarted his game. "You make a good point."

"Of course I do," I said as I picked my book back up.

"So…you think I'm a god?" he asked wryly.

"I think the swim team and the rest of the school think you're a god. Probably Percy Jackson's brother or something."

"Hey, I understood that reference." He just sounded so proud of himself.

"And I understood that reference," I said and we shared a smile.

"You got a thing for America's arse, do you?" He was grinning widely.

"Who doesn't?" I replied. "It's a very nice arse."

"So, you're an arse girl. Good to know."

I snorted. "Depends on the arse."

"How can it depend on the arse? That makes no sense."

"It does. Some guys, you can judge them on their arses. Some you can't."

"What else do you judge them on?"

"Well…" I thought about it. "If he's got a really good personality, it doesn't matter what his arse looks like."

Alex faked-gasped. "You mean there are personalities you don't hate?" he asked sarcastically, but he was smiling to show no harm intended.

I didn't take any. I smirked. "There are."

"Name one person in this school you don't dislike."

I could have been teasing. I could have been rude. I could have been a great number of things. Instead, I told him the truth for some unfathomable reason.

"You."

This time, when his controller dropped into his lap, he was so surprised he didn't pause the game. "Really?"

I smiled at him and it felt soft and sincere. "Really. I don't not like you."

His eyebrows scrunched while he tried to work out the double negatives. Finally, he beamed. "You like me!"

"I didn't say that. I said I didn't not like you. There's a difference."

Once again, Alex's optimism wouldn't be deterred. "You like me," he said cheekily as he went back to his game.

I made a good show of going back to my book. "I didn't say that."

"Yeah, but you do."

Both smiling, we went back to our activities.

"Oh, hey, man," I heard Alex say after a little while. "Wanna hang?"

"Actually, I'm here for Lottie."

I looked up from my book and saw everyone in the room was on pause. Everyone being Alex, me and Birdman, who hovered just inside our dorm door.

Had I not known better, I'd have said that Alex looked panicked. Like he thought Birdman was about to ask me out and would really rather he didn't. But I did know better – Alex wouldn't care about that – so, at most, that was just surprise on Alex Landry's face and I knew just how well he liked to be surprised.

My first thought was that Birdman was about to ask me out as well. The premise was unbelievable but, once surmised, made the most sense. Why else would he want to talk to *me*? I wasn't the approachable kind. Which again had me circling back to no one would want to ask me out.

"Hey," Birdman said, giving me a nod. "Can, uh… Can we talk?"

I could do nothing else but nod. "Uh, sure. Come on in."

He took a few hurried steps forward, then shot a look at Alex.

Alex held his hands up and stood up. "All right. Fine. I know when I'm not wanted." He turned on his heel and stalked into his room, closing his door loudly enough to make a point but so as to not quite be a slam.

Birdman took another few steps towards me, then paused and started wringing his hands.

"Dude, relax," I told him, trying to lighten the mood that had overtaken the room.

He huffed a rough chuckle and ran his hand through his dark blond hair.

"Take a seat and tell me what you want to talk about," I said, patting the cushion next to me.

He nodded, surged forward, and folded his lanky frame onto the window seat beside me. "Okay, so...I..." He let out a breath and looked at me like he wanted me to tell him what was up.

"Can't help you if you don't give me words," I said, shrugging apologetically.

He gave a self-deprecating smile. "No. Right. Of course." Still nothing.

"If you're here to profess your undying love, then I'm going to have to let you down easy..." I warned him, not knowing how else to cut to the chase.

He laughed. A lighter chuckle like I'd actually

successfully managed to lighten the mood. "No. God, no. I mean, not that... Huh. Not for you anyway. Not that you're not lovely, it's just..."

"All good, Henry. You do not need to justify *not* having a thing for me. We are all good on that front."

He gave me a nod. "Great. I... So, I'm not normally... You know us, we're..."

"Usually a lot better at finishing your sentences?" I offered.

Birdman grinned. "Something like that." He breathed out heavily. "I was thinking about last week."

I frowned, not remembering what he could be referring to. "What about last week?"

"When Fret mentioned that you know about girls."

"If you'll remember, I also said I'm not as useful as you might think."

He smiled softly. "Yeah. But I'm still convinced you understand more than you think. I also value your opinion."

"You do?"

He nodded. "Of course. If any girl's like you, I think that's a good thing."

118

Well, it was difficult not to feel flattered. It was also difficult not to appreciate to him as a person, not when he seemed to appreciate me as a person.

"Naw, are we bonding?" I teased him, nudging him gently.

He laughed. "I think we might be."

I looked up at the ceiling and tried not to just smile like a goofy idiot. "Tell me about this girl then."

"She's on the girl's basketball team," he said.

I nodded. "Of course she is."

"She's so good, Lottie. And she's tall and gorgeous. And her smile! Damn, her smile."

His wonderment was making me feel a bit giddy myself.

"So, what do you need from me?"

He shrugged as he looked down. "I dunno. I guess I… Well, I have no idea how to talk to her."

"You are aware she's just a person, right?"

He looked at me and laughed. "Yeah, Lottie. I worked that out."

"She's not the Queen or some goddess, whatever the brain between your legs is telling you."

He snorted. "Pleasing image."

"Just be yourself and… Who's a girl you *can* talk to?"

He looked at me like I was supposed to know the answer.

"Right," I said with a nod. "Me. I'm a girl."

"Yes, you are," he chuckled.

"Right. Well, just pretend you're talking to me. Say hi. Ask her… I don't know. Ask her how her season's going or something?"

"Pretend I'm talking to you?"

I nodded. "Yeah. And, if that fails, just smile awkwardly and run in the opposite direction while trying to remember how to construct sentences."

"That's your girl advice?"

I shrugged and grinned. "That is literally what I'd do."

We sat in contemplative silence for a moment.

"Right," Birdman said finally. "Well, now I've got that off my chest, I'll leave you to your book."

He stood up and I felt like I was craning to look up at him.

"I assume it goes without saying that this was in confidence?" I checked.

He gave me a smile. "I won't make you swear any binding oaths or anything, but I'd appreciate it if you didn't mention it to the guys."

"You embarrassed you like a girl and worried she won't like you back?" I teased.

He was still smiling. "Just don't need their jokes before I really know what I'm thinking, I guess. Wait until I've decided I'm really into her before subjecting myself to all that."

I nodded. "Fair."

He started off towards the door.

"Henry?" I said.

He turned back. "Yeah?"

"I'm… If you want to talk about it more…"

He gave me a cheeky grin. "You'll risk social interaction for my emotional wellbeing?" he finished for me.

I nodded. "Something like that."

He tapped the couch before starting off for the door again. "Thanks, Lottie. I'll see you later?"

"Will do."

A few minutes later, Alex poked his head out of his

door, presumably to see if the coast was clear.

"So, you'll be friends with my friends, but not with me?" Alex teased as he emerged from his room again.

I grinned at him. "Anything to annoy you."

The smile he gave me in return looked very much against his will but would not, apparently, be fought.

"You'll deny it to your death bed, won't you?" he asked, still smiling.

"Oh, far longer than that." My tone clearly telling him I was being a dick for the sake of it. "You'll find me in the afterlife still denying we're friends."

"I'm like Jesus."

I snorted. "How?"

"You denying me."

"That would make me Peter. That seems a bit shit."

"How do you…? No. You know what, I'm not surprised you know that at all. If you don't want to be Peter, you know what you've gotta do?"

"Oh, yeah. What's that?"

He shrugged nonchalantly as he plopped back onto the couch. "Just admit we're friends."

"Are we though."

"We could be. You just gotta lean into it."

I smirked. "All right. Fine."

"Yeah?" he asked.

I nodded. "Sure. We can be friends. But I have ground rules."

He laughed, "Of course you do."

"We can be here for homework help and the occasional hang out–"

"And just generally be there for each other," he added.

"Yes, sure. And just generally be there for each other. But," I warned, my tone serious. "No falling for each other."

He crossed his heart as he shook his head. "No! No way. Not happening."

"No," I agreed. "We're so not each other's type."

He looked me up and down and nodded. "Definitely not each other's type."

I nodded as well. "Good. So no risk we'll fall for each other."

"Nope. We'll be just friends. For always."

"We've been friends all of five minutes, how do you know it'll be always?"

He grinned at me. "You know how you just know things?"

"No. I research and discover and learn."

"Yeah, you just know things. Well, think of this as something I just know."

"Your optimism is going to kill me, isn't it?"

The smile he turned on me was near blinding. "It might."

I huffed a laugh. "Great."

Chapter Ten

Jake and I had been messaging back and forth a bit. And when I say a bit, I mean *a bit*. It was all going fine until I was required to continue the small talk, then it all fell apart and the chat would stagnate for a while.

It didn't seem to bother him. He seemed to make a point of coming past my seat in the Dining Hall just to say hi now and then. Or he'd stop me in the corridor and we'd have a chat that involved a lot of hair tucking on my part, and coyly cocky smiles on both parts.

He was nice. He wasn't creepy. He seemed interested. That was the trifecta, really.

He wasn't the only guy hitting the trifecta in my life.

Alex was also nice. Alex was also not creepy. And Alex

also seemed interested. Although, as we'd well-established in our ground rules, interested in friendship. I think I regretted my decision to be his friend more often than not.

"Hi, friend," Alex sang one morning in Week 9 as I staggered out of my bedroom.

I shook my head. "Friends don't throw chipper optimism in friends faces before noon."

He laughed. "Friends don't let friends be grumpy."

I looked at him and realised my fierce glare probably just looked like barely-awake squinting. "Your optimism is legit just going to make me more grumpy."

"Is it, though?" he asked.

I nodded. "Yes."

"What if I told you I was accompanying you to breakfast?"

I smile despite myself. "You think that will make me happier about being awake?"

His smile was, unfortunately, infectious. "You're smiling. You're already happier."

Curse him. He was right. I still felt like I'd just crawled out of a bog and the blanket of drowsiness still hung over me, damp and clingy. But, inside, I felt lighter. I smiled because I felt happy. Tired, but being vertical didn't seem quite so bad after a few minutes talking to Alex.

So maybe I protested too much. Maybe – just maybe – the reason I told myself I regretted being his friend was just because I enjoyed having something to complain about. It might have also just not been used to having a friend who went out of their way to talk to me so much. Nor a friend who's first instinct was to try to make me laugh when I was in a major introvert mood.

It annoyed me that I appreciated that about him.

I realised I might actually miss him when we went on Easter break.

"You know what doesn't make sense?" I asked as we walked to the Dining Hall.

"I'm sure you're going to tell me."

"Easter."

He looked at me like I'd just suggested we have a daring threesome on the quad. "What? How?"

"It's meant to signal rebirth and new life, but that doesn't work for us. We're heading into Winter."

"What?" he repeated.

"Well, it all stems from the pagan celebration for Spring, doesn't it?"

"Does it?"

"Yes."

"Then why did you ask?"

"It was rhetorical."

"You're rhetorical."

I rolled my eyes. "As I was saying, Easter comes from the Spring equinox – the whole rebirth of Jesus thing – and it really doesn't work when Australia's heading into the opposite of new life and Spring and all that."

"How do you know these things?"

"I read."

He shook his head. "I'll rephrase. *Why* do you know these things?"

"I like knowing things."

"It is far too early in the morning for knowledge."

I scoffed. "Says the guy who gets up at the arsecrack of dawn and immediately functions like a human being."

Alex smiled. "It'll be before even the arsecrack next term after the clocks go forward."

"And yet, you still seem unbothered by this."

He spun in a circle with his arms out, nearly clocking a few people walking around us and grinning at them apologetically. "Look at all the bothers I give."

"Right on, Pooh," I muttered. "Still don't get it."

"It's for swim practice." He shrugged, like that explained it all.

"Are you a simmer because you're a morning person, or are you a morning person because you're a swimmer?" I asked him.

He was still grinning. "I dunno. *Porque no los dos?*"

Just hearing the quote had me salivating. I frowned at him. "I could really go for tacos right now. Thanks."

Alex smirked even wider. "Well, you're in luck. The boys and I are going out to dinner tonight. Zac's been pestering about it for weeks. You should join."

I looked him over suspiciously. "Like…on purpose?"

He huffed a laugh. "Yeah. Like on purpose."

"Are we allowed to do that?"

"You are actually allowed to hang out with me and my friends. They could even be *our* friends if you give them half a chance."

I wasn't going anywhere near 'our' anything. "I meant,

129

are we allowed to go to dinner?"

He nodded. "Yeah, Lottie. We're allowed off school grounds. Your mum would have signed a permission thing at the beginning of the year. We just have to sign out and be back by ten."

"That'll suit you and your grandpa bedtime nicely."

He laughed. Pure and joyous. "It does. Perfect excuse to be back home and in bed at a reasonable hour. Come on, though. We'd love to have you."

I shook my head, then flailed my arms up. "Okay. Fine. What else am I going to do on a Saturday night?"

He cheered, giving a whole lot more no bothers about who looked at him. "Yes! Brilliant. Okay, we're leaving at six."

I frowned as something hit me. "Just how far away is dinner and how are we getting there?"

"You shall see."

"Or you could tell me now?"

He shook his head cheekily as he headed for the food line. "You signed on. Just let the rest happen, *mon amie*."

"I'm going to regret this. I am so going to regret this."

"No regrets!" he whooped as we got our breakfast.

I had no choice but to smile at him and his antics. I couldn't help it. It wasn't just his smile that was infectious.

"There's a student garage?" I asked, looking at the cars.

Alex nudged me. "There's a student garage," he said excitedly.

I nodded. "Of course there is."

Birdman clapped his hands together. "We're gonna need to take two cars."

"Where are we going?" I asked.

Zac grinned at me. "You'll see."

"Yes," I muttered. "So, I've been told."

"Who's driving?" Fret asked.

Alex laughed. "I vote the two of us with our Ps."

Fret nodded. "Makes sense. Shotgun Zac's front seat!"

"E, you coming with me?" Alex asked.

For a moment, something quite close to a *something* zinged between us. I wasn't sure what kind of something it was, but there was the potential for it to be a something else. I chose not to look too closely at it, but the small attention I paid to it suggested it was a nice something.

By the time the boys had argued over who was sitting with who, Alex and I ended up in his car together and the others all went in Zac's car.

"This is the first time we've been out," Alex told me as we drove along behind Zac's car.

"That's comforting."

Alex laughed. "Not the first time we've driven. Don't worry, Zac and I both got our Ps in the Summer holidays. It's just the first time we've put it to good use and escaped school."

"I thought you liked school?" I asked him.

He smiled. "I do. I love school. I was catering to you."

"I don't hate school," I said.

He shrugged. "Not now we're friends, no."

I laughed. "Of course, because the world revolves around you."

"You noticed, too?" he asked, full of cheeky sarcasm. "I thought it was just me."

I smiled as I watched the bush wiz past us. It was almost

Easter holidays, but the sun was still going to be up for a little longer.

"So, how long do I have the pleasure of your company?" I asked him.

"It's about a half hour drive."

"And are you expecting me to talk to you the whole way?"

"You? No," he teased. "I'm surprised you've talked to me this long." He threw me a grin to emphasise the friendliness of the joke.

"I talk."

"Rarely."

"Enough."

"Debatable."

"I can carry on a conversation for half an hour."

"Yeah, but...can you?" he joked.

"What do you want to talk about?"

"Tell me about your latest book."

"We have half an hour, not half a day."

"Is that all it takes?" he laughed. "Good to know how to get you talking."

"It's really not rocket science."

"You're not rocket science."

"Glad you noticed," I sassed.

He laughed again. "Come on. You've got a book to tell me about."

So we spent the half hour drive with me telling him about my current book, which so happened to be the last in a trilogy, so I had to give him all the backstory for the rest of the series. He very politely listened to me prattle on the whole time, interjecting only with a couple of questions.

As we got out of the car after he'd parked, he said, "Okay, so I might need to borrow that from you."

"You can read?" I fake-gasped.

He grinned ruefully. "I can."

"If I'd known you were going to read it, I wouldn't have given up so much of the plot." I'd pretty much given him a play-by-play.

He shrugged. "I like spoilers. Makes me not worry about where the story's going to go."

"But that's half the fun!"

"Half the stress."

"Reading shouldn't be stressful."

"That's probably why I don't do it very often."

I smirked as we met up with the others. "So, where are we going?"

"The café," Zac said excitedly as we stopped outside a door. "They've got everything!"

"They've got a decent selection," Birdman amended, holding the door open for me.

"The nachos might not be tacos, but they're *so* good," Fret told me.

"I like the hot dogs," Alex said.

We found a seat and Birdman passed me a menu while they all talked about what they wanted.

"It's tradition to come here on the way home," Luke explained to me.

I nodded. "Fair enough. Must be good then."

"It's the closest café to school. Even if it wasn't any good, we'd still come here."

The way these boys ate, I wasn't surprised at all.

"Double chips?" Alex asked, looking at me from the opposite side of the table. "I assume you're going to steal mine."

"I might get my own," I replied.

"Yeah, but will you?"

Looking over the menu, I thought the burger sounded the best. "Well, I'm thinking burger, and it says it comes with chips."

Alex nodded. "I'll get extra. For when you're done with those and need more."

"Just how much do you think I'll eat?"

"When you try these chips?" Birdman asked. "All of them."

They weren't wrong. The café chips were the best chips I'd ever had. And I didn't think the company or the atmosphere had any bearing on that, despite the fact that both were actually awesome.

Hands and arms crossed the table as everyone passed condiments and serviettes to each other or stole chips from each other even when they had plenty on their own plates.

Soft drinks and laughter flowed freely as we talked about school and sports and books and home. I learnt about the boys' families and friends, and didn't hesitate to tell them about mine. We shared stories of our lives pre-Acacia and what we wanted to do post-Acacia.

Three hours flew by and finally Alex was spluttering

between laughter, "Okay, we gotta get home before we get ourselves grounded."

We all staggered back to the car, so hyped up on laughing that we looked drunk. I couldn't remember a time I'd laughed so much or so hard.

Luke, Fret and Birdman all piled into Zac's car with Fret moaning, "Oh, I might be sick…"

"Well, you shouldn't have had that third pizza," Luke said.

"If you throw up in my car, I will leave you on the side of the road," Zac threatened.

"If you do that, he'll die and then who'll clean it up?" Birdman pointed out.

As he got into his car, Zac thought about that. "Fine. You'll have to spend the rest of the trip in the boot."

Alex and I laughed as we headed for his car.

"So, was that so bad?" he asked me, his arm brushing mine. "Hanging out with us on purpose?"

I nudged him softly as we walked. "It wasn't. Thanks."

He gasped sarcastically. "Did Elliott actually enjoy social interaction."

I snorted, but had to admit it. "She did, Sasha. Let's not

make a habit of it."

"No," he chuckled. "God forbid."

As I dropped into bed that night, I felt like something significant had shifted in my world. No longer was I Lottie the Loner, future swamp witch extraordinaire. No. I'd been kidnapped and adopted by my roommate and his overly confident and extroverted group of friends. It wasn't intimidating. It wasn't really against my will. I found it comforting and felt, surprisingly, good to belong.

Chapter Eleven

Mum had been there to pick me up at two on the dot on our last day of term.

I'd spent the whole evening before pestering Alex about what I was supposed to take home with me and what I was supposed to leave behind. He'd laughed at me mercilessly, but helped me pack.

He's also insisted on meeting my mum in person. And she was just as charmed in person as she'd been over Zoom. They'd talked for a full half an hour before I'd been my usual wonderful self and insisted we go. Mum had gently berated me, but Alex had just laughed it off as 'typical Lottie behaviour', because of which I'm pretty sure Mum decided she loved him.

"Alex seems nice," is what she said to me as we made our way along with a whole bunch of other cars making their way away from Acacia Academy.

I nodded. "He does *seem* nice, doesn't he?"

Mum threw me a side-eye. "Is he not nice to you?"

"Oh, no. He's very nice to me. By which I mean, he's so nice he's annoying."

"Aw," Mum cooed. "Did you make a friend?"

"I made five," I huffed.

"Yay!" Mum cried loudly in the small space, making me jump.

I tried not to, but I laughed. "Does that count as joining something?"

Mum looked at me askance, almost like she couldn't believe who I was.

"What?" I asked.

She shrugged and failed to hide a smile by looking straight ahead. "Nothing."

"Not nothing."

"I just don't remember you quite so quick to laughter," she said quickly before continuing, "Now, count as joining something? How often do you see them?"

140

I was happy not to go into anything that resembled me laughing more easily. "I see Alex every day."

"How often do you hang out with them?"

"Like how often does our club meet, kinda thing?" I sassed.

Mum smiled. "Yes. That exact thing."

"Alex and I actively hang out probably every few days. The other boys…at least once a week. They all took me to dinner the other night."

Mum was silent for a while, then she threw me a smirk. "They're all boys?"

"Ye-es," I answered slowly, wondering where she was going with it.

"And they're all…just friends…?"

"Yes," I said definitively. "They are all just friends. They're all sports jocks. Totally not my type."

"I don't know," Mum said in an almost sing-song. "It's not that big a leap from friends to more."

I rolled my eyes. "Life is not a rom-com."

"No, but you *are* hanging out with jocks. So, who knows!"

"I know," I told her. "Just friends."

"Fine," she huffed. "Is there a boy?"

"Why is it always about boys with you?" I laughed.

"Elliott, if you have children, you will soon discover that they come to an age where you have no idea what to talk to them about. If that time comes, you'll resort to something that you hope has the best chance of being safe and the smallest chance of being considered 'out of date'. One thing that's almost universal is romance. Also, I'm really nosey."

I laughed again and slowed as I saw Mum's soft smile.

"In that case, there could be a boy. Maybe."

"Oo, tell me more."

"His name's Jake. He's in Year 12 and on the rugby team with Luke, one of my new friends."

"Is that how you met him?"

I shook my head. "No. He came and talked to me at Lunch."

Mum gasped sarcastically. "You mean he actually approached you unprovoked?"

I nudged her gently. "Shut up."

"Is your resting bitch face slipping, or he is unbelievably brave?"

I snorted. "To save face, I'm gonna say he's unbelievably brave."

Mum smiled at me. "That's my girl."

We spent the rest of the trip home – extended by us stopping for an early dinner/snack – talking about boys and school and work, and singing very loudly and mostly off-key to songs she grew up with and I'd been forced to listen to all my life. Time seemed to fly and it made me realise that I'd missed Mum more than I'd thought. It was nice to catch up with her in person.

I spent the holidays much busier than I'd anticipated.

I saw Flick and Leah and Marsh more often than I did before I moved schools. Needless to say, they weren't too pleased I hadn't told them about rooming with Alex earlier. They forgot about it by the time I was telling them about Jake and they'd caught me up on their lives and the life I'd left behind.

I hung out with Mum at work a bit. It wasn't the first time I'd spent the holidays at the library since Dad had died, and they liked to keep me busy. They were also a captive audience for my fangirling over the Acacia library. Finally, people who understood.

There was also the compulsory dinner with my dad's parents so they could hear all about Acacia. They approved of my enthusiasm for the learning and the library, pleased that I appreciated 'quality' when I experienced it. As per Mum's suggestion, we didn't tell them about the dorm allocation mess. I just told them that my roommate was nice and we'd become friends. They were more pleasantly surprised by that than I thought they had a right to be.

Messages flew between me and other, real humans. Not only was Alex messaging me just between the two of us, but he'd added me to a group chat with the other boys so that my phone was dinging most of every day with stuff flying back and forth. And I actually responded way more often than I'd have thought me capable.

Jake was also exchanging messages with me. Not nearly as often as the others, but with a regularity than had me wondering how a relationship with him would work.

I'd learnt he was one of the farm kids, living only a couple of hours from school. That put him about three hours away from me when making good time. Sure, I could see him most of the year. But how did you even date at a boarding school? I made a metal note to ask Alex if it was ever necessary. Time would tell on that one.

Before I knew it, two weeks was over and it was back to school for me. Between everything that had gone on, I'd managed to sit the test for my Learner's permit, so Mum even let me drive some of the way. That added an hour or so to our drive.

Mum helped me haul my bags with all my freshly laundered clothes up to my dorm and we said our goodbyes. This time, I promised her I'd give her a call. I think she liked that.

"Hey, you're here," Alex said with a smile as he walked into the dorm room.

I nodded. "I made it back safe. Just had practice?"

He grimaced. "Yep."

"How was it?" I felt like he wanted me to ask.

"Froze my ruddy bollocks off." He did a little jig like his bollocks needed reassurance or whatever it was that bollocks needed or wanted.

"I'd have thought the exorbitant fees covered things like pool heating," I remarked.

"Oh, they do, wisearse." But he was smiling as he said it. "But it broke over the holidays and was only turned back

145

on last night."

"I assume it takes a while for it to heat the pool, then?"

"A couple of days this time of year."

I looked at him. "Wait a minute. Why do you even have practice now? It's a Winter term."

He nodded. "Yeah. The Acacia Angelsharks do all the Swimming SA competitions, even over Winter. Next one's on the twenty-third."

I searched him, not sure why he'd lie. It'd make a pretty shitty prank or joke or whatever. Finally, I had to conclude that, as bizarre as that sounded to my non-swimmer brain, it must be legit.

I shrugged. "All right, then."

Term Two was markedly different to Term One.

Namely, as I went to sit at my empty table end for Lunch that first day back, two people took hold of one of my arms each and steered me towards a different table. I still had my tray in my hands and I looked from side to side to find Luke and Birdman – not surprising as they were the tallest of the boys.

"You guys quite all right?" I asked them as they finally hovered me over a chair and gracefully dropped me into it.

Birdman nodded. "All good," he said as he dropped beside me.

I looked around the Dining Hall to try to get my bearings. "I'm at your table. What am I doing at your table?" I asked the boys as more of them dropped into seats around me.

Zac, Fret and Luke sat across from me and, finally, Alex sat beside me. He gave me a companionable elbow as he settled.

"What is it you like to say?" Alex mused. "The extroverts are kidnapping your introverted arse. You're ours now."

"I'm yours now?" I looked around at them, one eyebrow raised in question.

"Not, like…ours…" Fret said quickly.

"But like…us…?" Zac didn't sound sure. "Ow!" he snapped at Alex.

"Did you just kick him?" I laughed at the absurdity of it all.

"We had a plan," Alex hissed at Zac and Fret. "Stick to the plan."

"The plan was to kidnap me and make me yours?" I

asked him. "Cavemen, much?"

Alex rolled his eyes. "You pedant. Ours, like our friend. Like one of us." He gestured to the other boys. "Like we're each other's people. You know?"

I appreciated the sentiment. Three months ago, maybe not. But Term-Two-at-Acacia-Lottie appreciated it. I definitely appreciated Alex's word use. Who knew he knew what a pedant was?

"You're saying you're my people?" I clarified.

Alex nodded, seemingly very proud of himself. "Yes."

"Whether I like it or not?"

"Is that not the only way introverts get themselves friends?"

I had to give him that one. It wasn't the *only* way, but it was the most common. What kind of introvert would I be if I didn't get adopted by a bunch of extroverts at some point in my life? Now was just as good a time as any.

I sighed. "All right. Fine."

"Fine?" Alex asked, a smile dying to get out but hesitating in case I changed my mind.

I nodded. "Fine. You've convinced me. You're my people."

"That was a lot easier than I expected," Fret said as he stole one of Birdman's chips.

Birdman smacked his hand. "Why didn't you get your own?"

Fret pointed to his tray. "But, noodles."

I nodded again and pointed at Fret. "Dude has a point."

Birdman looked at my tray. "You gonna steal my chips, too?"

I smirked. "Nah. I've got Alex's," I told him as I took a chip off Alex's tray.

"Oi!" he cried.

I shrugged and gave him my best coy look. "I thought you were my people?"

"And that means you get to steal my chips?"

"Um…" I pretended to think about it. "Yes."

Alex muttered under his breath, but it was too low for me to catch. Then he nudged me and grinned. "I'll get double tomorrow."

Birdman laughed. "You would finally use your charm for extra chips, and you do it for her?"

Alex shrugged. "We kidnapped her, it seems only polite to treat her well."

Birdman nodded. "Yeah, okay. Fair point."

And it was like that every day. If I even hinted that I was going to sit in my old spot – out of habit rather than spite – I'd be gently steered to their table. No one in the rest of the school made a mention of it. They didn't look at me weirdly for it. It was like, in reality, nothing had changed. I'd made new friends and the world had gone on regardless. Who'd'a thunk it?

On Friday, there was a strange voice at the dorm door. "Hey, Lottie is it?"

I looked up from my typical window seat spot. There was a girl standing there. One I might have seen around but certainly didn't know. She was obviously dressed up. Casual, but nice casual. It hadn't got too cold yet that her dress was completely inappropriate for the weather. My assumption was that Alex had another date. Didn't hurt to not make assumptions, though.

"Uh, yeah. Can I help you?"

"I'm looking for Alex."

I nodded. "I'll find him."

It wasn't like there was terribly many places he could be. He was either in his room or in the bathroom.

I uncurled myself and saw the bathroom door was closed. I knocked on it.

"Yeah?" Alex called through the door.

Established protocol the term before dictated that 'yeah' meant it was safe to open the door and 'hang on' meant 'do not under any circumstances open that door unless you're ready to see something you couldn't unsee'.

I opened the door and found him doing his hair.

"Super classy getting the girls to pick you up for dates," I quipped.

He grinned at me through the mirror. "What can I say? I'm a classy kinda guy."

I shook my head. "She's here. Shall I tell her you'll be…another two hours?"

"Har, har. No. I'm all good." A couple more tweaks of his hair that made no discernible difference and he stepped away from the mirror.

I nodded. "Good."

Alex and I left the bathroom, me to my window seat and him over to the door.

"Hey," he said, all suave sophistication. "Sorry to keep you waiting."

The girl smiled and gushed, "No worries. I might have been early."

"Shall we?"

She nodded. "Sure."

"I'll see you later, E," Alex said to me and I looked up from my book long enough to catch his eye. "I expect you to have not moved."

I stuck my tongue out at him. "Funny. Have a good night. Behave."

The girl giggled at my suggesting they'd get up to anything. I found I didn't care for it.

As Alex and the girl left, I had the weirdest feeling I could have cared he was going on a date with YET another girl. But I decided it was just as well we were only ever going to be friends, because then I didn't have to care that he was apparently incapable of forming a romantic attachment.

Chapter Twelve

"If you were going out with me, would you prefer to go to a party in the Eucalyptus House rec room, or the movie night in the Wattle House rec room?"

I looked at Alex, who was hovering in my bedroom door, an uncertain look on his face.

"There's a party in Eucalyptus house?" I asked.

Alex nodded. "On Friday night."

I thought about it for a moment, then realised what he'd said. For some reason, I was in a shit-stirrer mood. "I'd rather sit in the library."

"To what? Watch you read?" he chuckled.

I gave him a look. "No. Privacy."

I could almost see the gears in Alex's head turning.

"Oh," he said, then the lightbulb went off. "Oh!"

I nodded. "Yeah. Oh," I said with a smile. "Who are you going out with now?"

"Hm? Oh, Sarah."

"Do I know who Sarah is?"

"I dunno. Do you?"

I frowned as I thought about it. "No. I don't think I know a single Sarah."

"Then, no. You don't know her."

We shared a smile.

"Did you ask Sarah what she'd like to do?"

Alex looked like the thought hadn't actually occurred to him. "Ask her?"

"Do you, like, just make all the decisions about these dates?" I asked him, not sure I wanted nor needed the insight into his dating habits, but finding myself morbidly curious.

He shook his head. "No. Sarah just asked if I wanted to go to the party or the movie night. I said yes. I kinda assumed she wanted me to choose."

I popped a piece of chocolate into my mouth. "Both events are chaperoned, yes?"

He nodded. "Of course they are."

I tried to envision what you did at a chaperoned party at your boarding school. "Well, what kind of date do you want?"

"What do you mean?"

I rolled my eyes. "I don't know why I'm surprised. You say you date so much so you can get to know them and decide if you like them, yeah?"

He nodded again. "Yeah. How else will I know?"

"Okay. So where will you be able to get to know them more?"

He clicked his fingers at me. "Party."

"There you go."

He went to leave, then paused. "What if she wants to go to the movie."

"Then you go to the movie," I told him.

Alex looked like I was maybe bullshitting him, then his blooming smile dropped. "Is this girl advice?"

"It's whatever you want it to be, man. Don't come to the chick who doesn't date and ask her for dating advice."

He grinned. "Yeah, good point."

"Rude." But I gave him a cheeky smirk so he knew I

was only joking.

He gave a ridiculous little chuckle, then sauntered off.

"What are you doing tonight?" someone asked, coming up behind me in the Dining Hall line at Recess on Friday.

I turned and saw Jake standing there. "Firstly, hi," I said.

He grinned. "Hi."

"What am I doing tonight?"

Jake nodded. "Yeah."

"I don't have any plans. Why?"

"I thought you might want to hang out?"

I smiled at him. "Did you?"

He smiled back. "I did. What do you think?"

"If you invite me to the Eucalypt party or the Wattle movie night, I'm going to say no."

He laughed. "Okay. Good to know. What do you want to do?"

I shrugged as I grabbed some food. "Alex is out. You could come hang in our dorm?"

I still didn't know where Alex and Sarah were going, but I reminded myself it didn't matter.

Jake nodded. "Sounds good. After dinner?"

"Sure."

"It's a date."

"Oh, is it?"

Jake gave me a lop-sided grin. "Can it be?"

I pretended to think about it as we got to the end of the line. "Yeah. It can be."

"Cool. I'll see you then." Still half-behind me, his hand touched my back softly and he pressed a quick kiss to my cheek.

"See you then."

We headed off for our own tables as I found Birdman as I went.

"Were you just talking to Jake Harman?" he asked, taking a chunk out of an apple.

I gave him a coy smirk. "I might have been."

"Do I need to give you boy advice?"

"Are you going to tell me that boys just want to get in

my pants?"

He laughed. "I was going to tell you that boys want to get into your pants, but that most of us are terrified of it."

"You're terrified of it?"

He nodded. "Yeah. What if we don't know what we're doing? What if we're bad?" He leant towards me, putting an arm around my shoulders. "We don't even know what we're going to find down there."

As we got to our table, I looked at him sceptically. "What do you think we've got down there?"

"Down where?" Zac asked.

I noticed Alex looking between me and Birdman's arm around me and couldn't guess what was going through his mind. Birdman let go of me and sat down.

"Between our legs," I told Zac as I sat down as well.

"Whose legs?" Fret asked, apparently having a 'who can shovel more food into their mouth' competition with Zac. Unsurprising.

"Girls," I answered.

"Oh, I hear it's got teeth," Fret joked.

I rolled my eyes. "It hasn't got teeth."

"Yours might not have teeth," Zac said seriously, then

broke out into a grin.

I knew it was pointless to argue with them because they were taking the piss after all.

I was glad when it became obvious that Birdman wasn't going to say anything about me talking to Jake. Maybe it was payback for me not saying anything about him having a crush but, given the boys' propensity for taking the piss out of the simplest things, I was more than happy to keep it to ourselves for a while longer. I finally fully understood not telling them until I knew what I thought about Jake.

Later that night, I was standing in front of the mirror in my room and wondering if I was dressed right. I hadn't done a lot of dating. Most of the incidences that even came close to a date were group dates; Flick, Leah, Marsh and me going out with a few guys from school and not being sure exactly who liked who, but hoping the guy you liked didn't think he was out with your friend. Sometimes, I was pleasantly surprised.

I'd chosen a fairly typical button up shirt and pants combo, and added a knit jumper to the mix because you can take the girl out of the library but you can't take the library out of the girl.

My hair was sitting in its usual mess of curls that I had no inclination to do anything about.

Finally, I shrugged. "He asked me out. This will have to do."

Because I had a tendency to be ready for things early – provided they weren't happening in the morning – and because Jake and I hadn't specified a time, I was standing in the living room wondering how much time I had before he arrived. Alex had already gone for his date, so I pulled out my trusty book and curled up in my window seat.

"So, this is what you do when you're being?" I heard Jake's voice and looked up.

"Usually, yeah," I said, uncurling myself again. "Come on in. Welcome to our…abode." I waved my arm around the room.

Jake nodded. "Looks the same as my dorm."

I tucked my hair behind my ear. "Are you in Banksia House, too." I hadn't even looked, despite numerous perusals of his profile since he'd first messaged me.

"Nah, over in Eucalyptus."

I nodded, wishing for quite possibly the first time in my life that I was better at small talk.

"You wanna sit?" I asked.

Jake nodded and we dropped onto the couch.

"How's rugby going?" I asked. I had zero interest in rugby, but thought it a polite and safe question.

I suddenly understood what Mum had meant about safe topics of conversation. What she'd neglected to add was that safe topics were likely to be boring ones.

"Couple of weeks in, can't complain," he said with a smile.

I nodded. "Good."

"How about…?" He paused. "Your stuff?"

I tucked my hair behind the other ear. "Stuff is good, thanks. Yeah. Fine. Homework and whatnot."

"Cool."

We sat in silence for a while, kind of nodding. I didn't know if I'd infected him with my lack of social skills, or if he already lacked them.

"Do you want to watch a movie?" I asked finally.

If we weren't going to talk and it seemed a little premature to call an end to the whole thing, then we may as well do something.

"Sure," he said. "What do you wanna watch?"

161

For some reason, Alex popped into my head. "'Fast & the Furious'?" I suggested.

Jake looked surprised for a moment, then gave me a smirk and nodded. "Sure. Sounds good."

"What's that look for?" I asked him as I put the movie on.

"Nothing," Jake said. "Just surprised you're into that."

"I'm into a lot of things," came out as though I was definitely suggesting something raunchier. I wasn't sure how I felt about that, but it could have been worse.

A little bit into the movie, Jake did the old arm behind my back thing. I had to wonder if boys watched more rom-coms than they'd probably admit to. Where else were they getting the ideas for all those clichéd moves?

Clichéd or not, by the end of the movie, I was kissing him.

As far as kisses went, it was fine. It was nice. Enjoyable. I can't say there were fireworks but, considering I'd never felt fireworks or anything close, I wasn't even convinced fireworks existed.

"Oh, uh…" I heard Alex's voice and gently pushed Jake away.

"Hey," I said to him with a nod.

Alex looked, for quite possibly the first time in his entire life, taken completely off-guard and not in a good surprise kind of way.

"Landry, right?" Jake said to him.

Alex just nodded like he'd lost the ability to do anything else.

"Did you want a picture?" I teased.

Alex shook his head. "Uh. What? No. I'm fine. I'll leave you to it."

He looked like he was going to turn and leave, thought better of it, then looked like he was going to head to his room. Only, he didn't go anywhere.

"All good," Jake said, getting up. "I should probably head off. Curfew and all."

I looked at the time and saw that it was after ten – so, late for Alex – which meant that the only places we were allowed to be was our own rooms or the rec rooms, as opposed to other people's rooms. It didn't actually stop kids being in other kids' dorms, especially on the weekend but, when members of the opposite sex were involved, it was better to be safe.

Of course, that didn't count for me and Alex, but Miss Fairley had done her job and popped in on us unsuspectingly numerous times, so maybe it was better to encourage Jake to leave rather than stay.

"Okay," I said, giving Jake a smile. "I had a nice night."

Jake gave me a nod, but looked like he was keeping a wary eye on Alex for some reason. "Me too. I'll see you later, Lottie."

"See ya," I said and gave a ridiculous little wave as Jake walked out.

Alex and I stood there for a few moments.

"So, uh…" Alex said slowly until he was sure Jake was out of earshot. "How do you…? I didn't know you knew him…?"

"My life does go on when we're not together, you know," I told him as I resettled on the couch.

He didn't join me.

"No. I mean, I know." He nodded quickly with his mouth pursed in this kind of 'is this a believable smile that says I'm taking this seriously?' impression.

Who was this adorably flustered boy in front of me?

"So…you and Jake, huh?" he asked, but he sounded a

little bit stilted.

"What? You jealous?" I teased.

The silence was just a little too long that I looked at him quickly.

He scoffed, "Pfft, no. Of course not. Why would I…? No. Surprised is all."

My immediate instinct was that he was jealous. But that was stupid. Why would Alex be jealous of me kissing Jake? He wouldn't. That was just my imagination. But why would my imagination come up with Alex's jealousy? I didn't want him to be jealous. That was as ridiculous as the idea of him being jealous.

"Of course," I said. "Just surprised. Because I'm not the kind of girl who'd kiss a boy."

"That's not what I meant," Alex said earnestly. "I just didn't know you knew…"

I didn't know if he was having trouble saying his name, or if he thought it was too rude to finish his sentence.

"Jake?" I finished it for him.

"Well, kinda. Anyone other than us, really."

"Am I not allowed to be friends with anyone else?"

He shook his head so quickly I was worried about

whiplash. "No! By which I mean, be friends with whoever you want. You don't need anyone's permission."

The mood between us had suddenly got very weird and I wasn't sure why or how.

I cleared my throat. "Good. No. I didn't mean to... I didn't think you... You know."

Alex nodded. "Yeah. Exactly. I wouldn't... Certainly didn't mean to..." He cleared his throat, too. "So, uh, 'Fast & the Furious', huh?"

I nodded. "Yeah. Yep. Want to watch the second one?"

He paused.

"Or are you going to bed?"

He looked at his bedroom door like bed was calling to him. Then he looked at me and somehow seemed to have the same look.

"No. Sure. Let's watch it. You want ice cream?"

"You've got ice cream?"

"I've got ice cream."

I nodded. "Sounds good."

I got the movie ready while he pulled the ice cream out of the freezer. It wasn't the best freezer, being as it was a compartment to the fridge, but it kept ice cream at a semblance of hard. Once procured, along with two spoons, he sat down next to me. By the very nature of a lack of crockery in our dorm, we had to both eat out of the tub. It occurred to me that, minus the current mood in the room, that wouldn't have seemed weird to me.

I tried not to let it seem weird now.

I hit play on the movie and we settled in against each other to watch it.

It took all of ten minutes before the mood broke and things felt back to normal. Normal being that we started a sword fight with our spoons and cracked ourselves up.

"On guard," Alex laughed.

"On your guard, sir," I said with a smile.

We spent the rest of the movie arguing over whose spoon got preference in the tub, elbowing each other playfully, and finally Alex fell asleep against my shoulder. I didn't have the heart to move him until the movie finished, by which time I had a bit of drool on my jumper.

Chapter Thirteen

A couple of weeks later, and things hadn't been weird again. Not between me and Alex at least. I hadn't heard much from Jake. I didn't know if it was because he didn't think the date was much of a success either, or if he felt weird about Alex.

Either way, if he wasn't feeling it, I wasn't going to lose any sleep over it.

"I need a condom."

I swivelled in my desk chair to look at the body who'd barged through my door.

"Uh huh. And you think I have one?"

Alex waved his hand around aimlessly. "There was the guy on the couch…and…"

I grabbed a pillow off the bed and threw it at him. "Just what kind of girl do you think I am?"

He shrugged. "The normal kind. The normal kind normally have condoms."

"What the hell's wrong with the one you're seeing tonight then?"

Alex smirked. "Not the normal kind."

"Oh, watch out. You might fall for this one."

His scoff was of such self-reassurance that I re-evaluated my entire existence. "Of course I won't."

All I could do was blink.

"Now. Have you got one?" he pressed.

I was still blinking, but I was regaining higher brain function.

"Uh, yeah…" I said, trying to remember where I'd put it.

I'd never been in a situation where I needed one. I had no plans to be in a situation where I needed one in the near future. But I'd promised Mum I'd have one 'just in case'. Logically, it was sensible. Things happened. I got that. And someone may as well make use of it before it expired.

I opened my bedside table and fished out my bag.

Calling it a handbag made me feel about a hundred, and calling it a purse made me feel even older. While Alex waited none too patiently, I rummaged for the condom.

"Here you go," I said as I held it out to him, then I pulled it back. "Don't be stupid."

Alex looked at me with the same exasperated fondness one looks at their parents when they give the same warning.

"Oh, my God," I whispered. "I've turned into my mum." I looked up at him and brandished the condom. "Do whatever you want. Go nuts. Have a great time."

He laughed. "Okay. Will do." He took the condom from me. "Thanks, E!" he called as he headed out.

After he'd left, I just sat in my room for a bit and mulled over whatever had just happened. I wasn't sure what I expected Alex to get up to on his dates, but I had to admit the idea he was having sex on them…surprised me. Maybe it was just because I was having a hard time working out where he was doing it. But I'd already acknowledged that teenagers were nothing if not a resourceful lot.

That had to be it.

I was just surprised because it hadn't occurred to me.

There was absolutely no other reason I might be feeling weird about it.

Chapter Fourteen

The boys were in our dorm room early on Sunday. I could hear them from my room. Made sense, baseball and basketball were over until Term 4, and rugby and soccer were both on Saturday.

They were being their usual raucous selves and, for once even still half asleep, it made me smile.

"She been out with Harman again?" Birdman asked.

"Not that I know of," I heard Alex reply.

"He said anything?"

"Nope." That was Luke. "Haven't heard a peep. Which is weird. Those guys usually talk."

"He's probably intimidated by Alex," Zac laughed.

"Yes," Fret said sarcastically. "The behemoth is scared

of the twiglet."

"Oi!" Alex cried and I heard Fret's 'ow'. "Speak for yourself."

"Maybe he sensed the tension," Zac said ominously and I grinned to myself imagining his expression.

"What tension?"

"Between you and Lottie," Fret said.

"There's no tension between me and Lottie," Alex scoffed.

"Well, there's tension between her and someone," Fret sang. "And it's not Zac."

"Oi!" Zac cried and there was another Fret 'ow'.

"There's no tension between her and anyone," Alex said shortly.

"Okay, calm down," Birdman chuckled. "She's going to have tension with someone someday."

"Fine. But no one here." Alex's tone was fairly final.

"You sure you're not protesting a little hard there, mate?" Zac asked.

There was a distinctive thump and a Zac 'ow'.

"Lottie's different. She's not…tappable. She's one of us. Always will be. End of story," I heard Alex say.

"Geez, mate," Birdman said. "All right. One of us. Enhance your calm, dude."

"My calm is enhanced. I couldn't be more calm," Alex said.

"Tell that to my butt bone," Zac's muffled mutter was only discernible because I'd snuck to my door to hear them better.

It took a few moments for things to sound like they returned to normal out there. I realised I actually had to pee quite badly, but thought it maybe a little too early to go out there. I didn't want the boys thinking I'd heard them.

Instead, I lay back down in bed with my book and furiously ignored the need to pee for another hour. By the time I deemed it safe to exit my room, my bladder was fit to bursting. There wasn't even going to be time to change.

"Hey, Lottie," Birdman said.

I held up a hand and gave them a, "Hang on," as I hurried to the bathroom as fast as my protesting bladder would let me.

I came back out and gave them all a smile. "Hey, guys."

"When you gotta go, you gotta go," Zac said knowledgably.

"Yes, thank you," I said to him, but I was still smiling.

"You're not dressed," Alex said, like it was some marvellous revelation.

I looked down at my PJs. "No. Not."

"When you gotta–" Zac started, but Birdman pushed him off the side of the couch.

They were all looking at me, Alex a little more intently than the others, and I was suddenly very aware I wasn't wearing a bra. Not that I had the biggest worries in that department, but it *was* cold and my PJ top *was* clinging to me.

"I'm going to go and change, then. Did I miss breakfast?"

Fret nodded. "It's almost Lunch though."

I gave him a nod in return while trying to surreptitiously cover my fripples. "Excellent. I'm starving."

I wasn't, but it was something to say as I slid back into my bedroom.

A few minutes later, I was back and Alex was the only one who looked at me. He kicked his chin in greeting, and the movement must have alerted Zac to my return.

"Can you come take over for me and kick his arse?" Zac

asked me, his tongue hanging out as he concentrated.

I sighed. "Fine. Let me have your controller," I said as I went over to him.

He kept furiously mashing buttons as he lifted the controller towards me so his avatar wouldn't get wailed on more than absolutely necessary.

"God, you're not…" I muttered as I took over for him. "You're not going to beat him that way."

"You think you've got what it takes?" Alex asked me.

"Oh, you're going down, Sasha," I promised him.

"Hey, hey," Alex protested. "Keep it clean, Elliott. There are minors in the room."

I smiled, but said nothing more as I was too busy making sure I whooped his butt.

"Best of three," Alex said.

By the time I'd won 'best of fifteen', it was Lunch time and we all trooped down to the Dining Hall together, Zac and Fret leading the way as usual. Alex was chatting with Luke behind them. Birdman and I were bringing up the rear.

"How you been?" I asked him as we wandered.

He nodded. "Yeah. All right. How about you?"

I also nodded. "Same old."

"Good to hear. Seen any more of Jake Harman?"

I didn't have to wonder why he was asking me that. "Nope."

"Date no good?"

I shrugged. "I just don't think there was any chemistry. You know?"

"Yeah," he said, almost sadly.

"Things not gone well with Basketball Girl?" I dared to ask.

He smiled. "They haven't gone badly."

"Have they gone at all?"

He looked ahead at the boys playing funny buggers as they were wont to do. "Yeah, not really," he chuckled.

"I'm sorry?" came out more like a question than a statement.

"Thanks," he laughed. "It's fine. I can just admire her from afar."

"How very renaissance of you," I said with a smile.

"Come on, you two!" Zac called from the door to the Dining Hall.

I noticed that Birdman and I had fallen even further

177

behind.

"Coming!" I told the excitable ball of food-obsessed goodness that was Zac Parker.

As usual, Zac and Fret had an eating competition to the point I wasn't the only one concerned that Fret was going to throw up.

"Take him home," Alex laughed and Luke and Birdman walked to overfull others back to their dorms.

Which left me and Alex dropping onto the couch in our dorm by ourselves.

"Why don't you go out with Lara again?" I asked him, completely out of the blue for both of us. "She seemed nice."

"Why?" he laughed. "Because she didn't tell the whole school about my non-existent crotch injury?"

I shrugged, but smiled. "Sure."

"Did she ask you?"

"Did she ask me what?"

"Did she ask you to get her another date?" he asked.

I wrinkled my nose. "No. Why would you think that?"

"Because why else would you bring it up?"

It was a good question. Why else would I bring it up?

Why would I possibly care whether Alex had the staying power for more than one date-slash-hangout-slash-whatever he called it?

"Do the girls not care you only go out with them once?"

Having kept myself to their little party of five, I had no idea what the rest of the school thought about Alex's one date policy.

Alex shrugged. "They don't seem to. Way I see it is this, right? You don't know if you like someone until you spend some time with them. Proper time. Not just some flirting in the school corridor."

It wasn't the first time he'd made the proclamation.

"So you're just sampling the available options?" I asked cynically.

"Or, I'm open-minded enough to give anyone a chance."

I looked him over in a way that told him exactly what I thought about that.

He snorted. "What? What's wrong with that?"

"I'm just trying to decide if you're actually that open-minded or you use that as an excuse to play the field."

"*Porque no los dos?*"

179

"Seriously?"

"What? What is your hang up here?"

What was my hang up here? "Maybe if you're not looking for anything serious, you shouldn't…lead them on."

"What are we? Sixteen going on thirty?"

"That doesn't really give you an excuse to just date and dump every girl in the school."

"It's hardly every girl in the school, E. Why are you suddenly so concerned about my dating habits? You didn't seem to care so much when you were telling Lara about my crotch injury."

I didn't know why I suddenly cared so much. But, after talking about it more, I was feeling a touch indignant on behalf of the girls he dated.

"Maybe I care about you," was all the excuse I could come up with.

"I appreciate the sentiment," he said, leaning against me for a moment. "But I'll be fine."

If I thought about it, he'd been out with maybe four girls in the time since I'd started at Acacia. Which was what? Four months? Did that seem like a lot? I couldn't even tell anymore.

I'd seen him talking to Lara just that week and there seemed to be no hard feelings.

"How about," he said, "you worry less about my love-or-lack-thereof-life and focus your womanly ways on the boys and their girl problems?"

My eyes narrowed at him. Did he know about Birdman's crush? After not hearing about it for a few weeks, I'd assumed he'd decided he wasn't quite so interested in her as he'd originally thought. Maybe he hadn't said anything to me because he'd been talking to Alex.

"Who's got girl problems?" I asked.

Alex shrugged. "All of them. You see any of them getting dates?"

Now he mentioned it, I realised that the boys didn't get dates. Everyone at the school seemed to like them, they were charismatic and nice and funny, and they were a decent-looking bunch of boys. At any other school or in any of my rom-coms, they would easily have a date every weekend if they wanted one.

"I'm sure they'd have dates if they wanted them," I said.

181

Alex waved his head non-committally. "Maybe."

"You think you're the only one who's got any pull with the *ladies*?" I teased.

He elbowed me playfully. "Not when you put it like that. No." He nudged me again, more gently this time. "If it makes you feel better, I'll keep it in mind."

I suddenly felt a bit weird and wondered if I wasn't supposed to have an opinion at all. Were he Flick or Leah or Marsh, I'd probably have said the same thing to them and not felt weird about it. Surely it was just something friends said to each other. Showed concern for them and whatnot. But with Alex, I suddenly second-guessed me bringing it up at all.

So I shrugged. "Sure. Whatever you want."

Whether Alex heard the something weird in my voice, he just laughed and said, "Great. Thanks."

Chapter Fifteen

I was in the library doing some research for an assignment. My happy place. But then, if it was my happy place, why did my mind keep wandering?

I'd left the dorm while Alex was at practice, so I hadn't seen him that morning. It had been a good excuse for a tummy not quite ready for food to avoid breakfast, so I hadn't seen any of the boys either.

It took me a moment, but I realised I missed seeing them. Missed seeing the people who I could be busy exclaiming how annoying hanging out with them was while we all knew I secretly liked having them around. It wasn't like I didn't feel like I could be myself with Flick, Leah and Marsh, but I wouldn't have been able to bemoan their presence and have them take it as the mostly-joke it was. They just weren't like that, and that was okay. But Alex and his…our friends, were and it made for a nice change of pace.

"There you are," a voice said and I looked up to see Alex walking towards me.

I'd camped out against the wall at the end of one of the aisles.

"How'd you know where to find me?" I asked him with a smile.

"Well," he said as he sat next to me. "I thought to myself, 'where would Lottie be?' and I was like, 'giant nerd hangs out at the library'. So, here I am and here you are."

I nudged him companionably. "Here I am. How was practice?"

He nodded, running his hand through his still-wet hair. "Fine. Wet."

"How're your bollocks?"

He laughed and nudged me back. "Also fine. Heater's been working perfectly since it was fixed."

"What a relief," I breathed.

He chuckled. "Nice to know you care about my bollocks."

"Only because I know how much the mean to you."

He barked a laugh. "Yeah…"

"Why is that?"

"Why is what?" he asked.

"Why do your…bits mean so much to you? You're always so worried they're too small or not right. What's up with that?"

"Hit me where it hurts, why don't you? Way to give a guy a complex, E…"

"No," I said. "Sorry. I don't mean you personally. I meant guys in general."

"Oh, well in that case…"

He threw me a look and we shared a smile.

"I dunno," he said finally, looking around at the books on the shelves. "Maybe society tells us that's what's important? Maybe it's because it's one of those things we're not supposed to flash around? Everyone's unsure of the unknown." He looked at me. "Aren't you ever worried about your boobs?"

I shook my head. "No. They're annoying as much as

anything. I suppose, when I was younger, we went through a phase of being worried we'd never get them when it felt like everyone else was. But I've never been worried about the size or what anyone else thought about them or anything." I looked down at them. "Maybe that's weird, though."

Alex looked down as well. "Well, I think they're fine."

We caught each other's eye and I was pretty sure we were both blushing.

"Not like…fine," he said quickly. "Not fine like good. Fine like…adequate."

I tried to fight the smile. "Adequate? You think they're adequate?"

He shrugged, looking at little nervous. "Was that not the right thing to say?"

"If I told you your dick was *adequate*, how would you feel?"

"Decidedly not," he answered without hesitating. "Sorry…"

I gave him another nudge. "It's fine. I don't actually care. I just wanted to see you squirm."

"Oh, you…" he muttered, then tickled me.

Laughter burst out of me until I clamped my hand over my mouth and managed to bat his hands away.

"We're in a *library*, Sasha!" I mock-chastised. "Have some respect."

"Respect? Oh, I'll show you respect, Elliott," he threatened with a smirk.

Just before his fingers touched me again, one of the librarians appeared at the end of the aisle with a disapproving glare that I was sure they handed out upon one's appointment of library custodianship.

I was batting Alex's hand away from me as she put her finger to her lips and hissed a sharp 'SHHH' in our direction. For good measure, I nodded to her.

"Sorry, we'll keep it down," I whispered loudly.

"See that you do. The library is not a playground," she said, then turned on her sensible heel and walked away.

Alex was still trying to poke me, but must have only been only half-heartedly because his finger was easy to block.

"If you get me thrown out of the library..." I warned him while trying not to laugh and be very serious.

"What will you do to me?" he asked, not trying to hide

his laughter at all.

"Oh, you don't wanna know what I'll do to you, Sasha."

He leant towards me and said, "Maybe I do, Elliott…"
like some kind of cowboy in an old Western.

It was at that point that I realised how close we were to
each other. Our noses were almost touching. My hand was
in his from where he'd been trying to stop me blocking his
pokes. We were looking deeply into each other's eyes and
I saw the smile in his. It would be so easy for one of us to
just inch that bit closer and kiss the other one.

Which I thought was a very weird thought to have.

Neither of us wanted to kiss the other one. We were just
friends. Good friends, I'd come to accept and actually be
happy about, despite and protestations to the contrary.

And yet, neither of us moved for what felt like a *very*
long time.

Finally, Alex said, "Uh…so I came to find you to let
you know the boys were going to drop by this
afternoon…?"

"Was that a question or a statement?"

Alex's eyes scanned what little of my face he could see
from so close up. Then he pulled away slowly, leaving my

hand in his.

"Statement," he said with a humourless chuckle. "If that's okay?"

"So, a question?"

He looked down at our hands like he was surprised to see them connected. "Kinda?"

I shrugged. "It's your dorm, too."

"Exactly," he said. "Too. I didn't know if you were planning on being here all day, or…?"

I shook my head. "Not all day. I've got a bit more work to do, but then I might come hang?"

He gave me that crooked grin. "You'll come hang? On purpose?" he teased.

"If you try poking me again…" I said, again failing at very serious and trying not to laugh.

Alex gave my hand a squeeze and finally let it go to stand up. My hand suddenly felt quite cold and lonely.

"We'll see you in a bit, then?" he asked, humour still all over his face.

I nodded. "Sure."

His look got more serious, but his eyes still shone. "You can't miss lunch *and* breakfast."

"How do you know I missed breakfast?" I asked, fake-indignantly.

"Because I've met you before."

"All right, fine. I will come and drop my books off in time to walk to lunch with you all. Happy?"

He nodded. "Very. Be quick, lunch starts in…" he checked his fitness tracker watch, "like an hour."

I nodded as well. "I know. I know. And Zac and Fret wait for no man."

"Or woman," Alex added.

"Or woman," I agreed, nodding again. "All right, begone with you and I'll see you soon."

He chuckled, nudged my foot with his, then jogged off.

I swore that boy couldn't do anything lazily.

I finished up what I was doing, and got back to our dorm room in a little over an hour.

"Oh, but she's so beautiful," Fret was whining, lying on the couch with his hand over his eyes.

"What's wrong with him?" I asked.

"Boy's got a crush," Birdman said.

I looked at him and we exchanged a knowing look. I wasn't going to narc on a friend, but it was rather pot

190

calling the kettle black.

My eyes swivelled to Alex and I noticed he was looking between me and Birdman quickly as though his brain was trying to tell him something, but as though he didn't know what it was.

"What?" I asked him.

Alex shook his head. "Nothing. Hey! You can help Fret with his girl problems."

Fret sat up and looked at me pleadingly. "Oh, please, Lottie!"

"How am I supposed to help?" I laughed. "I don't even know who his crush is."

"Kayla Barrett," he sighed wistfully, melting back onto the couch.

Well, that was more than Birdman had given me. I didn't even know who the basketball girls were to begin trying to work out who she might be.

"She doesn't even know he exists," Zac offered, only to be smacked by Luke.

I dropped my books on the kitchenette counter and wandered over. "So how can I help?"

Fret was busy sighing wistfully on the couch.

"Dunno," Zac said. "I suggested he just ask her out for this Friday, but she'll be going to Girls' Night."

Girls' Night. I did know all about Girl's Night. It was like some mini girls-only semi-formal. A chance for the girls to get all dressed up and have somewhere to go. The bottom floor of Callistemon House was finished and it was going to be a sort of grand opening of their Rec Room. Apparently, the rest of the building was taking somewhat longer.

I looked at Fret and all I felt was sympathy. The guy just really liked this girl.

"How would I even ask her out?" Fret sighed.

All the boys looked at me.

I shrugged. "What? It's not rocket science. You say, 'you wanna go out sometime?' Easy as." I pointed to Alex. "Ask Alex, he seems to get enough dates."

"Yeah, but Alex never asks them."

I looked at him in surprise. "Really?"

Alex nodded. "Yeah. What? Why? Is that weird?"

"That you've never liked a girl enough to ask her out?" I clarified. "No. Not at all."

"Hey," he said, full of indignation. "The whole point of

a date is to get to know them."

I waved my hand dismissively at him. "Yes, I'm aware," I said, more shortly than I'd intended.

What did it matter to me if he couldn't work out if he liked people or not?

"I know Kayla," Fret sighed. "She's kind and funny and nice and sweet and *so* smart."

"Don't tell me she's also on the girls' soccer team?" I asked.

Fret frowned at me. "What? No. She doesn't do a sport. She plays violin."

Wow, the guy really did know her. I was going to make a stalker joke, but the look on his face told me it wasn't the time. I, of all people, knew how much you could learn about people from just watching them. In a not at all creepy way, of course. It was called paying attention. Or people watching and, even though I had my head in a book as often as possible, I also liked people watching. From a safe distance, they fascinated me.

"I can't ask her out anyway," Fret moaned.

"Why not?" I asked.

"Not yet."

"Why?" I repeated.

"She doesn't know me. Why would she say yes?"

I looked him over and my brain sped through the list of reasons to reassure him. "Because…" I started, hoping something good would come to me. "You're kind and funny and sweet, too. Why wouldn't she say yes?"

Fret looked at me. "Do you think?"

I had no idea. "Sure. If you're feeling a bit weird about it, why don't you introduce yourself next time you see her? Then you can chat to her a couple of times before you ask her out?" I offered, feeling like that was a legitimate strategy.

Fret grinned. "Yeah! Yeah," he said, getting more enthused by the second. "Thanks, Lottie. I'm gonna do that!"

He leapt up and started heading for the door.

"You're going to do it now?" Alex asked.

Fret shrugged, a big smile on his face. "It's lunch, I know where she'll be."

He found Kayla in the Dining Hall and made a beeline for her.

"Damn," Birdman whistled to me. "I wish I had his

confidence."

I nudged him gently. "You do, you just have to remember that."

"Naw," he teased. "Was that a compliment?"

"Don't tell the others," I told him. "They'll all want one."

"Your secret's safe with me." He gave me a wink.

Alex looked at us like he'd caught the end of the sentence and was suddenly worried about what he was missing out on. He said nothing about it, though.

Later that week, Fret had successfully struck up a budding courtship with Kayla, but was still finding it difficult to just ask her out already.

"All right!" I sighed heavily on Thursday at Lunch. "All right."

All the boys stopped talking and turned to me in question.

"Fine," I said. "I will infiltrate Girl's Night and see what I can learn about this…Kayla person."

There was silence as they all looked at each other, then back to me.

"You know that means you'll have to, like, dress up and

shit?" Alex asked me carefully.

I glared at him. "I'm well aware. Thank you. But I'll do it if I have to."

Alex and Birdman were grinning like cats who'd eaten all the cream.

"You only think you have to because we're your friends," Alex sang.

"Naw," Birdman joined in. "You like us."

"I'm doing this for Fret," I clarified, pointing at each one in turn. "Just for Fret!"

Fret threw his hands in the air. "She likes me!"

I dropped my head in my hands and sighed, but the smile wouldn't wipe off my face.

Chapter Sixteen

I didn't know why I'd agreed to this, much less been the one to suggest it!

I'd been hurrying backwards and forwards between the bathroom and my bedroom, trying to remember how to dress up nicely. There was a reason I wore tights or pants at every available opportunity. I hadn't worn a dress or skirt with naked legs in years – so thankfully all my schools had had either pants and/or year-round tights options.

"You don't have to shave, do you? Inclusivity and all that," Alex called.

"No, I don't *have* to," I called back. "I *want* to. Personal choice and all that. My pasty pale legs aren't usually on show!"

I came back out of the bathroom in just a towel and found four sets of surprised eyes and Alex being very much 'eh, I've seen it before'.

"Sorry," I mumbled, then dashed into my room again.

"Are you okay, Lottie?" Birdman asked.

"Leave her be, she knows what she's doing," Alex told him.

I poked my half-dressed person out of my room long enough to say, "Actually, I don't know what I'm doing. I don't do all this girly shit. You owe me big for this!"

Rationally, I knew I wouldn't hang this over any of them. I'd suggested it and I was willing to do it for Fret, but I was in a panic about getting out of my comfort zone. It had never been something I'd been particularly good at, and just the idea alone seemed to give me weird anxiety.

Finally, I was dressed and coifed and supposedly stunning. If you believed Flick when she'd talked me into not only buying the dress but also packing it for boarding school because, in her words, 'you never know when you're gonna need to slay'.

I didn't feel like I was going to slay, but I also

recognised I was perhaps not the best judge of my personal appearance.

"Oh… You *can't* go looking like that," Alex said when I walked out of my room.

I looked at him incredulously, anger bubbling away to a rather persistent boil.

"Excuse you?" I asked.

"Duuude…" he whistled. "You look *so* uncomfortable."

I shook myself out and wobbled on my heels. "I am. Thanks for pointing it out."

Zac was shaking his head. "You can't go."

Fret was also shaking his head. "Even for love, I can't let you do it."

None of them thought I looked even half decent?

I looked down at myself. "I look *that* bad? Gee, thanks guys."

"No," Birdman said. "You look *amazing*. On the surface."

"But just so…not you," Zac said.

"Just super uncomfortable," Fret agreed.

"Go put your starchy button up back on. Cook can be

the girl," Alex said, pointing at him.

Luke beamed. "Really?"

Alex shrugged. "Why not?"

"I've always wanted to know what I'd look like as a girl."

"Have you seen your sister?" Zac asked and got thumped for his troubles by Alex.

"You know who Kayla is?" Fret asked, because of course the only thing he was concerned about was whether the mission was accomplished.

Luke nodded. "Yeah. I know her."

"No!" Fret cried. "If you know her, she'll recognise you."

Luke rolled his eyes. "I don't *know her*, know her. I know who she is."

"How are you going to get past the teachers?" Birdman asked.

He shrugged. "I'll make it work."

"That's nice and all, but what about clothes?"

"Drama department has a bunch of stuff that'd fit him," Zac suggested.

Alex went into leadership mode. "Okay. Birdman and

Zac, go to the Drama department and find him a wig and an outfit," he said.

The two of them nodded and headed off.

"You're going to trust them to pick out an outfit?" Luke asked.

"Birdman, yes. Zac's just there for the breaking and entering."

"Good point." Luke nodded.

"Now we just need to get Luke in makeup."

"Will I need to shave my legs?" Luke asked.

Alex looked at him quizzically. "Did you want to…or are you asking if you have to?"

Luke shrugged. "Either."

"You're going to shave your legs for a one-night only dress-up party?" I asked Luke.

He looked at me quite seriously. "Why not? You did."

I blinked. "Touché, sir."

"All right," Alex said to him. "Go and de-hair yourself."

"I'll get my makeup back out," I said, kicking off my heels and wandering to the bathroom.

Once Luke was washed and shaved and coiffed to the

nines, he strode out of my room like he owned the bloody joint. Heels and all.

"I still can't believe you found heels to fit him," I said with a shake of my head.

"I still can't believe you made him look so good," Alex said to me.

And, Luke did look good. He made a surprisingly feminine girl. It made me try to picture what the other boys' female counterparts would look like.

"Just because I don't care about that stuff, doesn't mean I don't know anything about it," I answered.

Alex smiled. "I wasn't throwing shade. Imagine not knowing…I'm a swimmer, then challenging me to a race. You'd be pretty freaking surprised when I beat you so well."

I nodded my head in thought. "Yeah. All right, I guess."

Alex nudged me companionably. "Exactly. I might have to get you to do my makeup for formal," he teased.

"Oh, you coming, Lottie?" Luke asked.

I looked between them all, waiting expectantly for an answer as they were. "Uh, I don't know. I'm still thinking about it."

"You should totally come. It'll be a great night," Zac said.

"How would you know?" Birdman asked. "We've never been before."

Zac nodded. "Sure. But everyone knows the Green and Grey is top shit."

Alex wrinkled his nose. "I wish they had a better name for it than that. Royal Green would be way better."

"Don't the girls' schools call them 'Royal's?" Zac asked.

The boys all looked at me.

I held up my hands. "I am not a font of all female knowledge!" I laughed. "I don't know these things. I was public before I came here. Anyway, Luke has to get going!"

"It's Bonnie," he said.

"All right, Bonnie, get ye to the ball," I said, ushering him out.

He gave us a little flourish of his hand and sauntered away. We all stuck our heads out of the door to watch him walk down the corridor.

"He's hot," Birdman said.

"Hotter than his sister," Zac commented.

"I just hope this works," I said as I trudged over to the couch and dropped into it, still dressed up myself.

On one hand, I felt like a bit of a failure. Wasn't the girl supposed to do the big transformation and the guys thought she was the most beautiful thing they'd ever seen? What was wrong with me that I couldn't even pull that off? I guess it showed they cared about me more than just for my pretty face. That thought cheered me up a bit, but I still felt like I'd failed on the girling-front somehow.

Chapter Seventeen

Eventually, we'd had to pack it in before we'd heard anything from Luke-Bonnie about the success of the mission, but we heard about it the next day.

"She's interested," Luke said at breakfast the next day, still with the remnants of eyeliner visible.

"Have trouble getting it all off?" I asked him.

He nodded. "Secret?"

I shrugged. "Yet to discover it."

He nodded more resignedly. "Fair enough."

"Back to the important stuff," Fret insisted. "She likes me?"

Luke nodded as he started shovelling breakfast. "Yep. Thinks you're cute."

"How did you do it?"

Luke grinned. "I didn't have to do anything. It just came up and I heard her. You know girls talk about guys *a lot*, right?"

The boys all looked to me for confirmation.

I nodded. "This is true. One would think we had nothing better to do."

Alex looked at me calculatingly. "I smell bullshit."

I shook my head. "No. Honestly. We talk about guys a lot. Guys we like. Guys we don't. Famous guys. Funny guys. Cute guys. It's like a whole thing."

"Huh," Zac said, leaning back in his chair. "What do you know?"

"Not much, obviously," Birdman said with a laugh as he pretended to sweep Zac's chair out from under him but caught him before he fell.

"What do I do?" Fret asked, eager to bring the conversation back to him.

"Now would be the part where you ask her if she wants to go out," Alex said, although he looked at me as though he was checking if that was right.

"If you want to go out with her, you've just got to do

it," I said.

"If it helps," Luke said. "I asked her what she'd say if you asked her out."

"And?" Poor Fret was beside himself with a mixture of excitement and terror. "What did she say?"

"She giggled and said she'd say yes."

"There you go," I told Fret as the other cheered. "Just go and ask her out."

Fret looked over to Kayla's usual table and nodded. "Just go and ask her out," he repeated to himself, like it was his new mantra.

He pushed himself up out of his chair, his face set with determination.

"Okay. I'm going to ask her out," he said.

"Go get your girl!" I said to him enthusiastically.

He gave me a distracted smile and stalked off.

"Did she really tell you that?" Birdman asked.

Luke gave us a shit-eating grin and shook his head. "No. She said he'd have to ask and find out. She did giggle though."

I shrugged as I ate some bacon. "That's usually a good sign."

207

"What is with the giggle anyway?" Alex asked.

I shrugged again. "Dunno. Maybe we think if we're cute, we'll be more likable."

"By who?"

"Whoever we're trying to attract."

"I do like a giggle," Zac admitted.

"You don't giggle very often," Alex observed.

I nodded. "I guess I'm not trying to attract anyone."

Alex looked at me for a minute and I looked at Alex.

Finally, he blinked and whatever connection we'd been holding broke.

"Well, Harman will be heartbroken."

I elbowed him playfully. "Shut up."

"What?" he asked innocently. "Maybe he really liked you."

"He's got a funny way of showing it," I said as Fret was making his way back to us.

"Well?" Zac asked.

"She said yes!" Fret squeaked, throwing his arms up and spinning.

He then dropped them quite quickly, looked around like he hoped no one had seen him, and dropped into his chair, making himself as inconspicuous as possible.

"She said yes," he whispered, beaming happily.

So, Fret had a date with Kayla and he was over the moon.

The next week, Birdman and I sat in class together – as we'd taken to doing – and I debated the sense in trying to work out who his crush was. After the success with Fret, I felt like Birdman deserved his own happy-for-now ending.

"So, it turns out I *could* help Fret," I said to him as the teacher went on at the front of the room.

He looked at me with a knowing smile. "That you could."

"Maybe I could help you, too?"

He grinned as he made a few notes. "Maybe."

"You've obviously thought about it…" I said slowly. "You came to me for advice before?"

He nodded. "That I did."

"Was it bad advice?" I asked.

He shook his head. "No."

"But you don't want any more of my help?"

"I didn't say that."

"You didn't say much of anything," I pointed out.

When did I become so invested in other people's lives in the real world?

"True," he laughed.

I thought I saw his eyes flick up quickly and not in the direction of the teacher. I looked around.

"Is she in our class?" I whispered, trying to work out which one it was.

"She might be," he said with a cheeky grin.

"Basketball... Basketball..." I muttered to myself.

"What are you doing?" he asked.

"Trying to work out who might play basketball."

"No one at the moment. It's winter season."

I rolled my eyes at him. "Yes, I know. But you *look* like a basketballer."

"What makes you think she does, too?"

I shrugged. "I don't know. Aren't people who are good at something or enjoy something supposed to look like it?

You know, like dancers *look* like dancers."

"I think you're thinking about dog owners. You don't really look like a book."

I stopped my search to look at him. "What would I look like if I looked like a book?"

"Dunno," he said with a shrug, then added thoughtfully, "Flat?"

I elbowed him a little less companionably. "How about that one?" I asked, pointing to a girl on the other side of the room.

He looked in the direction and shook his head. "No."

"That one?"

"No."

"That one?"

"Gee, we must have a lot of basketballers at this school," he teased.

"That one?"

"Why do you want to know so badly?"

"I actually don't know," I told him. "But I care." A horrible thought occurred to me. "Maybe I inherited my mum's nosiness?"

"There are worse things to inherit," he said. "Will you

lay off if I tell you?"

I nodded. "Definitely."

He looked around like he was worried someone was going to hear us. I mean, we'd been carrying on a conversation at the back of the classroom and no one had even batted an eyelid.

He pointed surreptitiously. "Zahra Dawson, okay?"

I peered ahead. I knew the name from rollcall and I vaguely knew the face that went with it. She was pretty. Tall and willowy with gorgeous black hair and tawny brown skin. Better still, from what I'd seen of her in classes, she had a brilliant brain on her. Whatever else Birdman was, boy had good taste.

I nodded. "Impressive."

"What?" he laughed.

"Substance *and* style. Colour me impressed."

He elbowed me now. "Shut up."

"No, really," I chuckled. "You could pick way worse."

"Like your good friend Liz Spencer."

I gagged. "Don't remind me."

It wasn't that I'd had run-ins with Liz Spencer. Words hadn't been exchanged. But plenty of looks had and, if looks could kill... I'd be slightly maimed and very much told off.

"Okay," I said. "How do we get you a date with Miss Dawson?"

He threw her a wistful look. "I have no idea."

Birdman and I took our new mission very seriously. Well, I was heavily invested and he was, at best, humouring me. Instead of hanging out in the library studying, I'd go and find him and try to get him to brainstorm things to say to Zahra with me.

Even if it took me weeks, I was going help him find the courage to ask her out.

We went for walks around the grounds.

We meandered between classes to talk.

We hung out in the rec room.

We hung out in either of our dorms, even without the other boys.

We talked about Zahra and life and school and our friends.

We spent a heap of good quality time together but, weeks later, I still hadn't managed to help him find his courage. Although, it turned it might not be courage he lacked, but rather self-esteem.

"I think she's interested in Angus Curry," Birdman said.

We were in the Banksia rec room, sharing a party bag of Doritos.

"So? You're not going to fight for her?"

He shrugged. "I'm not really the fighting type," he admitted.

I fake-punched him in the arm. "I bet you say that to all the girls."

He snorted, spraying a few Dorito crumbs.

"No?" I asked, feigning disbelief. "Pity. Personally, I'd fall for it." I put on a fake flirting voice that made Birdman smile.

"Fall for what?" Alex asked.

I turned to smile at him. "Nothing," I said.

Alex was looking between us again with that look like

his brain was trying to tell him something, but he couldn't work out what it was.

"What's up?" I asked him.

He shook his head. "Nothing." And then he left again.

"What's up with him?" I asked Birdman.

He was silent a moment, then shrugged. "No idea."

Birdman and I hung out for a while longer, then I headed back up to the dorm to find Alex gaming.

"Hey," I said to him.

He kicked his chin in greeting but didn't look at me. "Hey."

"You okay?"

He nodded. "Fine."

I nodded as well. As strange as his behaviour suddenly seemed, I wrote it off and curled myself up in the window seat with a book.

"Fret asked Kayla to the formal!" Zac excited voice interrupted me a while later.

I looked up to find him and Birdman at the door

"And?" Alex asked, expectantly.

"She said yes."

"Of course," Birdman added.

"Sweet." Alex nodded. "Who're you asking?"

Birdman shrugged, somewhat sheepishly in my opinion. "Dunno. You?"

I didn't know why Alex looked at me somewhat pointedly when he answered, "Probably Lara."

I felt a little…something at the sound of that. It was this little thing deep in my chest. It made me blink a couple of times and feel the need to force a smile. I wasn't quite sure what had come over me.

"Zac?" Alex asked.

"Vic Palmer," Zac said with a dazed smile.

I looked to the others for clarification as to who that was. The name was familiar, but I hadn't made a point to get to know people for a reason.

"Friend of your best friend, Liz Spencer," Birdman explained and I grinned.

"Oh, her." I nodded to Zac. "Good for you man."

Zac was grinning ear to ear, very pleased with himself. "We'll see you guys, later?"

Birdman nodded to me. "Dinner?"

I nodded back. "Sure. Sounds good."

"So…" Alex started when they were both gone again.

"So?" I asked.

"You and Birdman have been spending a lot of time together lately."

I snuck a peek at him. He was looking straight ahead at the TV, his fingers slowly and methodically pressing the buttons. Nothing gave away what he was thinking.

"I guess…" I said slowly.

"You guys seem to get along well."

I nodded. "Yeah. We do."

"Good. I'm glad."

I put my book in my lap. "You don't sound glad."

He shrugged and kept on playing. "No. I'm fine."

As though a lightbulb went off in my head, I worked out what he was thinking.

"Oh, no!" I laughed and that finally made him look at me. "No. Not that. We're just friends."

His expression told me he didn't believe me before he turned back to the TV. "Of course you are."

"We are," I said earnestly. "What? I can't be friends with him now?"

"You can be friends with whoever you like."

"Good. Because I don't see how it's fine I'm just

217

friends with you, but suddenly hanging out with Birdman has to be more."

Alex's controller took a bit of a thrashing. "Because it's Henry Bird. Nice, good, charming Henry Bird who'll unintentionally string you along and then where would that leave us?"

"Exactly where we are?" I suggested.

"No. It'll leave you not talking to us."

"To you."

"What?"

"You mean it'll leave me not talking to you."

"Fine. Yes!" he snapped like it was a hardship to admit.

I felt a little claustrophobic or something suddenly and needed to seriously lighten the mood. "You're not just projecting, are you?"

"What?" he asked again.

"You're not just worried that Birdman'll forget we're just friends because you're worried *you'll* forget we're just friends?"

For the tiniest blip of the shortest second, I wondered if that was exactly it. I also worried that my accusation of him projecting was me projecting. Was I at any risk of forgetting Alex and I were just friends? Was Alex at risk of forgetting? Were we both, together, at risk of forgetting?

The way we were looking at each other, I would have almost said yes.

But no. That was ridiculous.

It was so ridiculous that I scoffed out loud. At the same time that Alex scoffed out loud.

"No," he said, seemingly amused.

"No," I agreed. "Of course not."

"We're just friends."

I nodded. "That's it."

"Purely platonic."

"Definitely. Like not even vaguely interested in anything more."

"No. It would be stupid anyway."

"So stupid."

"Not even friends with benefits."

"Nope. No benefits."

"Benefits never work anyway."

"They don't. We'd either fall for each other–"

"Or hate each other," he finished for me.

I nodded. "And since we are most definitely not at all right for each other…"

"We'd just end up hating each other."

"Exactly. And there's no way I'm risking that."

"No. Losing you would be the worst."

"Total worst."

He nodded. "Good."

I nodded. "We're agreed."

"We are."

"We know where we stand."

"We do."

"Good."

"Good."

And with that sorted, we went back to our previous activities and didn't speak for the rest of the night.

Chapter Eighteen

Saturday was cold and wet and not much use for anything but movie marathons, hot chocolate and blankets.

Alex was at training, so I had the dorm to myself. Or, so I thought.

"Holy cripes, she's up before eleven!" I heard him laugh as he walked into the living room mere minutes into my movie.

"I thought *he* had practice?" I asked, wrapping myself back up again.

"He did, but coach is in bed with a sniffle so they cancelled it."

I heard him wander into his room, then back out again.

"What are we watching?" he asked as he jumped over

the back of the couch and landed beside me effortlessly in track pants and a hoodie.

I'd scooped up the popcorn just in time to save it being squished by his butt.

"I'm doing a 'To All the Boys' marathon," I informed him.

"And what exactly is that?" he asked, stealing some popcorn.

"Movie trilogy."

"Oh, I love me a movie trilogy. What number are you on?"

I paused the movie since it seemed like he wasn't going to go away any time soon. "The first one. Do you plan on staying?"

"Why wouldn't I? You going to share your blanket?"

It was a testament to how close we'd become in the last few months that I relented and gave up some of my very snuggly blanket for him. There was much dramatic and exasperated protesting on my part, but I was actually quite happy to do it.

"Awesome." He beamed at me. "Thank you. Now, what did I miss?"

I was all of twenty minutes in, so I just started it again for him.

"This is a rom-com!" he said a few minutes, sounding a combination of surprised and amused.

I looked at him. "So?"

"So, I thought I knew all your secrets by now."

I scoffed. "Oh, my secrets have secrets."

"Yeah. But, rom-coms, Elliott?" he teased.

I smiled at him. "Rom-coms, Sasha."

I loved rom-coms. Which was weird for a person who didn't really enjoy social interaction, to be so invested in the very definition of social interaction. After all, what was romance other than the ultimate in not just interaction but trust? It wasn't that I wasn't willing to go through that with or for someone. I'd just never found anyone I thought was worth it.

He nodded, smiled, and looked at the screen. "Rom-coms. All right. Bring it on."

Sometime during the second movie, he started having questions.

"That doesn't make sense."

"I thought she liked Peter?"

223

"Who even is this guy?"

Each time I elbowed him none too gently, gave him the minimal amount of answer, and shushed him. It didn't give him the hint to shut up. Not until the third movie.

"Ha! It's you!" he chuckled after Peter told Kitty he wasn't even allowed to talk once a movie started.

I elbowed Alex, but smiled. "You wanna talk, hit pause and I'll talk to you. 'Scuse me for actually wanting to pay attention when I watch a movie."

He grabbed the remote and hit pause. "I bet you're a HOOT on dates." He even hooted.

I rolled my eyes. "Duh. The trick is to go to a movie neither of you actually wants to see." I tried reaching for the remote again.

"Oh!" he exclaimed, holding it well out of my reach. "You sly dog, Elliott. Clever. I'll remember that one."

I smirked at him. "I bet you will."

A little while later, he hit pause again.

"What now?" I sighed dramatically, secretly pleased he was pausing before talking, although if it became a habit then it would take us hours to get through movies in future.

"What's so romantic about this?" he asked, pointing at

the screen.

"What do you mean?"

"I mean, what is the big deal? We wouldn't have this problem."

My brain shorted out. I found myself spluttering. "What? What do you mean *us*?"

He kicked his head towards the tellie. "You and me. Sure. I get it. It's sad. They're going to end up going to the opposite ends of the country–"

"You don't know that."

He gave me a look that suggested I rethink my statement. "They're so setting it up. They've been setting it up from the beginning."

I had to hand it to him. It was so going that way. Five minutes in, you knew it was going that way. "So? What's your point?"

"My point is, it's moot for us."

"What is this grand 'us' of which you speak?"

"Well," he started, totally matter-of-fact. "Our closest unis are in Adelaide, yeah? So, we'll be applying there. Closer and cheaper than the eastern states. No brainer."

"What if I want to go to Melbourne?"

"Do you?"

Well, no. I was a born and bred Adelaidean. I'd never consciously decided to go to an Adelaide uni, but I'd also never considered going interstate. The majority of us just didn't do that. We didn't have to.

"I might," was what I said to Alex.

"Pfft," he scoffed. "And pass up free room and board by living with your mum?"

I had to concede that one. "Yeah. Okay. I'm going to uni in Adelaide. But you don't have to."

He inclined his head. "But why wouldn't I? The courses are, for the generalised most part, all the same no matter what institution they put on your piece of paper at the end."

"It helps that Adelaide is one of the wine capitals of the world and a big chunk of wine research in Australia is done there," I noted.

He blinked. "How? How do you know these things?" he asked, and I knew it was rhetorical at this point.

I shrugged. "I know things."

He smirked. "Okay. Yes. In my case, there aren't that many unis offering my course. BUT! My point stands."

I had to give him that one. Maybe it was different in

other states. Maybe it was different in other social circles. But everyone I knew had gone to uni in the state they'd gone to school in. Everyone. If they moved, it was later. For work or romance, or both. Or Medicine. I didn't much mind being away from Flick and the others at Acacia for two years because it was assumed we'd all still be in Adelaide after that.

It was so weird to watch this movie, get heavily invested in it and the characters and their situations, but it be so different than what we were likely to experience. Was that the norm for US teens?

"Are all American YA romances just tragedies waiting to happen?" I heard myself whisper like I'd come to the epiphany part of a massive bender.

Alex snorted. "Oh, my God. I broke you."

I looked at him and I could feel how wide my eyes were. "No, seriously, Alex. Are they?"

He took my hand. "It's okay, E. Breathe." The chuckle in his voice wasn't helping.

"How in the hell do they ever *risk* dating?"

"Because why miss out on the good times, huh?"

I focussed on his face. "What?"

He shrugged. His thumb brushed over the back of my hand. "If you live in fear of losing something, you'll never really have it in the first place. And life is for living, Lottie."

I guess that made sense. "Maybe…"

"Come on. Why don't you reserve judgement until we've seen how this ends?"

He coaxed me back to relaxing on the couch and hit play. The movie was so darn cute and adorable that I lost all concern for the love-lives of random teens on the other side of the world and just enjoyed myself.

As the credits began to roll, Alex nudged me gently and I realised I was leaning against him. It felt more like an attention-seeking nudge and I didn't really want to draw attention to the fact I was leaning against him, so I stayed put.

"Mm?" I asked.

"Speaking of *prom*. Pfft. Ridiculous word. Formal?"

"What about it?"

"Any decision?"

"Yes."

Alex sat up quickly. "Yes!" he cheered.

I rolled my eyes. "No. Not yes going. Yes decision. As in decided no to going."

"Boo!" he cried as I got up to get another drink. "You *have* to come."

"I don't have to do anything I don't want to, Alex Landry."

He grinned at me over the back of the couch. I could see it in his eyes. "True. My bad. You *should* come. Please come."

"Need I remind you about the infiltration debacle? A girl like me doesn't do dances, Sasha."

He huffed. "A girl like you? What does that even mean?"

"A girl who can't get dolled up or look good in heels."

He waved a dismissive hand at me. "You can get dressed up without looking like a stuck-up princess wannabe. And the only person I know who looks good in heels is Cook."

Luke had pulled it off very well. I snorted as I passed him a drink and sat down. "I'm still not going."

"You know, my parents' place is like an hour out of Adelaide. Hour and a half tops. There's a local high school

229

nearby I could easily go to. But they chose to ship me off here and see me maybe a few weeks in the year, provided they're not on holiday when Acacia's on break."

I looked at him. "That sucks, Alex. Why are you telling me this now, though?"

He looked down at the drink in his hand for a moment. "Because everyone has their insecurities, E. Stuff our personalities – who we are – is built on, for better or worse. Mine is attachment. I get the concept, the benefits, but when it comes down to it, I avoid it to avoid getting hurt. I practised being charming so everyone will like me and hopefully not leave me. I can't stand to not be like or to be ignored or…even just not get on with someone. It's not all shallow, not the way you think. My real friends are few because that's all I can bear to trust. Romance is…so far off my radar."

I gave him a sympathetic smile. "Well, that's what you've got me for."

He grinned. "What's that, then?"

"I can't break your heart if I don't want it."

He nodded. "*Touché*."

I leant up against him again and he put his arm around

me companionably.

"If we all go to the formal together stag, will that convince you?" he asked as he pulled his phone out of his pocket.

I wrinkled my nose. "Ew. No. The others all have pretty, popular dates anyway."

"Nope. We're all going together. Stag. No girls allowed. Well…one girl allowed."

I laughed. "Thanks, but no. I'm not going to ask them to do that."

"You don't have to. I just did and they all said yes. It's a date."

I shoved him playfully. "Except it's not."

"Is that a yes, though?" he teased.

"Fret's not devastating Kayla?"

"That's between Fret and Kayla. He agreed."

What had I done to deserve not just the friends I'd left at home, but five new ones to boot? I knew there was only one option now. Especially if Fret was cancelling on his almost-girlfriend to go to the formal stag with me.

I sighed. "Fine. Yes. It's a yes. We'll all go together."

"Sweet. Hey, holidays coming up, perfect time to go

dress shopping!"

"Hooray," I mumbled sarcastically.

He probably wasn't wrong, though. It was Winter holidays in a few days. Three weeks at home. Mum would love to go dress shopping with me for my first formal.

"Ah, I'm going to miss that pessimism," Alex said wistfully.

I snorted. "Like you won't message me every day."

"Yeah, but that's not the same, is it?"

I had to give him that one. I'd noticed that, as the year went on, just messaging Mum wasn't cutting it. I'd even had a couple of video calls with Flick, Leah and Marsh. Nothing terribly interesting, just catching up.

"No. It's not," I agreed, leaning into him a little more.

Chapter Nineteen

I was back at Acacia Academy for Term Three and had to say I'd actually missed Alex over the previous three weeks, even though we messaged absolute nonsense at least twice a day.

He was the first one back this time and, as soon as I walked into the door, I was met by a hug.

"Lottie!" he cried.

"Are you drunk?" I teased.

Alex pulled back and looked at Mum. "Hey, Mary."

She smiled and patted him on the shoulder as she wheeled my suitcase past him. "Good to see you, Alex. Nice holidays?"

He shrugged. "Eh. It was okay."

"What did you get up to?"

"The annual family trip to Hotham."

"Oh, you ski?" Mum asked.

"Snowboard, duh," Alex said with a grin.

"Duh," Mum agreed.

"Lottie in the house!" I heard Fret cry and turned to see him and Birdman at our door.

"Hey, guys," I said with a smile.

"'Sup, Mrs Hopkins," Birdman said.

Mum smiled at them. "Mary, boys, please."

Fret bobbed his head. "Mary."

Birdman elbowed him. "How were your holidays, Lottie?"

I nodded. "Fine."

"Get a dress?"

"What dress?" Mum asked and I winced.

"Formal dress."

Mum turned on me. "You didn't tell me you were going to the formal! Lottie, it's in eight weeks! And I missed out on dress shopping?"

How she knew when the formal was, was beyond me. Woman probably read the newsletter front to back, then back to front in case she missed anything. I had to concede it probably just showed she cared.

I gave her a sheepish smile. "Sorry?"

She shook her head. "No. No Sorry." She pointed at the boys. "I'm going to Skype her and we're going to find something online."

The boys nodded like they weren't quite sure what they had to do with it.

"You make sure she doesn't pike out," Mum finished.

"Scout's honour," Alex said.

I rolled my eyes. "I'm sure that's blasphemous."

"It's not blasphemous," Mum said. "It's an honour code. Something I note you don't have."

"Because I forgot to mention I needed a formal dress?" I laughed, unable to take her incredulity seriously.

She nodded. "Yes. How am I supposed to live vicariously through you and revisit my shining youth if we don't go dress shopping?"

I smirked and she smiled.

"He wasn't even in the Scouts," I told her. "So it's all a lie."

"I can still uphold the Scout honour code," Alex said.

"Do you even know what it is?"

"I like to uphold the Pirate Code," Fret said, rocking back on his heels.

We all looked at him and smiled. He grinned back, seemingly quite happy with himself.

"All right," Mum said. "I think you're set. Just two more terms, then home again."

"Until next year," I reminded her.

"One year at a time, Ellie," she chastised, using my old nickname. "Right, been lovely to see you boys, but I'm due back in Adelaide before midnight."

"Why?" Fret asked. "What happens at midnight?"

Mum smiled. "I turn into a pumpkin."

I rolled my eyes. "Get out," I laughed.

Mum gave me a huge hug and a kiss and I helped her out of the dorm room.

"Lunch?" Fret asked.

I looked at my phone. "Bit late for lunch isn't it?"

Fret tapped his nose. "Not on Return Day. There's a long lunch."

"Why has no one told me this before?" I asked him.

Fret shrugged. "'Cos your roommate sucks," he

chortled.

I might have missed Mum while I was at school, but I certainly missed the boys while I was at home. It was nice to know though that after being away from one for a while, things were just the same as I'd left them.

"Hey, you got a condom?" I asked Alex later that week.

We were still trading condoms back and forth. I didn't know who he was using them with, or when, and I didn't care to find out. What he didn't know was that I wasn't using them and, when he asked me for one, I'd just give him back the one he'd leant me.

It seemed stupid for me to ask him, but I had this weird feeling that I needed to make sure he knew I was interested in other people. Other people being not him. It made little sense and I dwelled on it as little as possible. The drive was still strong, though.

"Yeah. Check my wallet." He kicked his head to the coffee table.

I picked it up and flipped it open to find it. It was where it usually was.

"Thanks," I said, wandering into my room.

Making sure he wouldn't see me, I slipped it into the

bag in my bedside table and went back to my homework until I needed to head to the library for a book.

I got back before I expected he'd be heading to bed, but I found him on the couch with a hot chocolate and watching tellie in his PJs.

"I didn't know when you'd be back," he said, "but I made you one. It's on the counter."

"Hey, thanks." I picked it up and dropped onto the couch next to him.

Accidentally, I'd dropped a little too close to him and our bodies were quite hard up close to each other's. He didn't seem to mind, so I just stayed where I was.

"What are you doing for next holidays?" he asked me after a bit as he put his cup down.

It felt awfully early to be thinking about the next holidays, considering we'd only been back a whole week, but then I did already miss Mum a bit.

I looked over at him. "Nothing much. I'll go home and Mum will have some weird and ridiculous plan of activities that we never would have thought of doing before I came away. Then, we'll spend all holidays rugged up on the couch in front of the fire watching movies."

"Sounds nice."

I nodded. "It is. What about you?"

"I'll spend two weeks at my parents' place probably by myself since uni holidays don't match up with school ones and my sister will be in the city."

That sounded like it would suck. "You could come down to the city…maybe?"

"Watch a movie by the fire with you and your mum?" he teased, then sobered.

I shrugged. "Whatever. We could go out. We could hang at home. Whatever we felt like. You could even stay over in our spare room, I'm sure."

"You inviting me home for the holidays, Lottie?" he joked, and this time the humour stayed.

It was then I noticed that he never referred to his parents' house as 'home'. He'd called Acacia home when we'd gone out to dinner in Term One. But he'd never called the one place that always supposed to be there for you 'home'. I didn't know if it was sad or not. I felt like I'd be sad if that was me, but Alex just seemed like that's what it was. I supposed it was one of those things he couldn't change so he wasn't going to get overly upset about it.

"Yeah, Alex," I said, keeping my tone as light as I could. "I guess I'm inviting you home for the holidays."

He laced his hands behind his head and smiled. "I'd love to."

Chapter Twenty

I woke up feeling like death. The reason for which was obvious about half an hour later.

So, I was tucked up on the window seat with a heat bag, some hot chocolate and my book for most of the morning. I was on my fourth hot chocolate when there was a very unfamiliar voice at the door.

"Uh, hey. Is Alex in?"

I turned and saw the stunning creature at the door. In comparison to the high levels of swamp witch I was giving off that day, she didn't make me feel all that great about myself. Or, that could just have been the period talking.

She looked too old for Alex but, unless she was a teacher – which I thought was beyond him, no matter how charming he was – she was at most a year older.

"No. Move on, sweetie. He and his commitment-phobia has, but don't take it personally…" I was full of less anger and more sadness as I finished, "he just doesn't want to get hurt."

"And how would you know that?" she asked me.

"He told me. But I shouldn't share it around so…" I held my finger to my lips. "Shh."

She just laughed. "You must be Lottie."

I looked down at myself. "In all my swamp witch glory."

She just smiled even wider. It was a smile I recognised. Something was ticking into place.

"I'm Marina. Alex's sister."

Well, that made a whole lot more sense. And explained why I recognised her smile. The family resemblance was small, but it was there.

"Oh, hey. Yes. Lottie is me. I am Lottie. Nice to meet you. Uh," I looked around in panic. "Alex is still at practice."

Marina nodded. "Figures. Okay if I wait? Aunt Tam said to make myself at home."

I nodded. "Sure…"

She walked in and lowered herself gracefully onto the couch.

There she was in a sleek skirt and shirt and coat with towering heels. Her hair was silky and wavy and so shiny, but good shiny. As I watched, she pushed at a perfectly placed wave like it was a tick. Like the way Alex kept training his hair up. She was gorgeous. Just as gorgeous as her brother, but in a different way. She reminded me of some posh New Yorker in a movie.

Then there was me in my over-sized comfy PJs and slouchy boot slippers. My hair in a messy bun with fly always everywhere because it wasn't actually long enough for a proper bun. I was ready to own my swamp witch destiny, but I was also a little bit awestruck at the put-together-ness of her.

"So, you're new this year?" Marina asked.

I nodded. "Yep."

"Did you board before?"

I shook my head. "No. Public school."

"Bit of a shock, I expect?"

I nodded. "Just a bit."

"Even more after being roomed with my little brother, I'll bet," she laughed. It, like, tinkled pleasantly.

"Ah, he's not been so bad. A surprise, yeah, but not so bad once we got to know each other."

Marina smiled at me. "He certainly has plenty of nice things to say about you."

That surprised me. Although, I wasn't sure if it was the fact he talked about me at all, or that when he did he had nice things to say. "Really?"

She nodded. "Yeah," she chuckled. "I'd have thought he was totally smitten with you."

I got a little burst of happy in my chest. "Really?"

"Yep. If he hadn't sworn up and down that you were just friends, that is."

The little happy didn't so much burst as dissipate. "Yeah. We're really not each other's type."

Marina looked me over. "No, I see that. Alex has rank taste in girls."

I laughed awkwardly. "I'm sure it's not…rank…"

"Okay, big sister exaggeration. He's still not got great taste."

I wasn't sure why that bothered me.

"Mare…?" Alex said, a question in his tone, as he walked into the room.

"Hey, little bro."

"What are you doing here and making yourself at home with my roommate?" he had the typical mistrust of a younger sibling expecting an older sibling to be in the middle of a prank.

"I'm here for your RSVP. Mum said no more dawdling."

Alex dumped his bag on the floor and sighed. "Ugh. Of course, I'll be there. It's Ilya's wedding." He looked at me. "Yep. Mum took her distant Russian heritage to heart when she named us."

Marina sniggered. "Foreign is sexy," she said in an exaggerated whisper, then looked at her brother. "It's not just yes or no. You know this."

For the first time, I watched as Alex stamped his foot. "I don't want to."

"You mean there's someone you can't charm your way around?" I sassed him.

He looked at me pointedly. "Do not get me started on my mother. Her and her bloody expectations."

"Appearances are important to her," Marina agreed. "We know this. We deal with this. It's legit just a person, Alex. Mum just wants you to bring a date."

I literally snorted. "Good luck with that."

Alex pointed at me, close to full-on tantrum-mode. "Even Lottie knows me well enough to know that's not going to happen."

Marina looked at her brother, then to me, then back to Alex, and back to me. "He can take you."

"What?" I asked as Alex cried, "Yes!"

I looked at him. "What? No."

"Why not? What's better than having my best friend there?"

While I liked the idea he thought of me as a best friend – the feeling was undeniably mutual if you tended to want to simultaneously hug your best friend and clobber them over the head – I wasn't sure that going to a family wedding was a very good idea. I had no idea why not. Maybe it was the need for a dress.

"Yes!" Marina smiled. "Perfect!"

I looked between them somewhat helplessly.

"Say you'll come. Please?" Alex asked.

"If you get down on one knee…" I started, feeling like he was so desperate he actually might resort to such kitsch tactics.

He crossed his heart. "Promise I won't."

"Will this get me out of the formal?"

"Not on your life."

"Can I wear the same dress?"

"You can wear a wine barrel for all I care."

"Alex," Marina admonished.

"She gets it," he told her, not taking his eyes off me.

I couldn't help but smile. If this was friendship, I could deal with it. If wanting to do something for someone even though you didn't really want to do it was friendship, then I already knew what my answer was going to be.

I nodded. "Fine. Yes," I laughed as he threw his arms up and whooped. "I'll go."

"Thank you!" He said as he wrapped me up and hugged me so tight my feet left the ground.

"See?" Marina said. "Was that so hard?"

He pointed at her. "Just make sure Aunt Tam knows there's nothing hinky going on. It's just a friend-date."

Marina's nose wrinkled. "Hinky? What? Have you

guys been bingeing 'Scooby Doo' or something?"

"Shut up," Alex muttered as he put me down and I laughed. "Did you drive all that way just to get me to bring a date?"

Marina shook her head. "I'm mid-work. We're trying to get a few more restaurant contracts so I'm the missionary."

Alex sniggered and I knew what he was thinking.

"Gross," Marina said. "Grow up."

Alex snorted as he tried to hold in his laughter. "No. Sorry. All grown."

"Anyway, I'm having brunch with Aunt Tam. You coming?"

Alex shrugged. "She didn't mention anything."

"Why would she? We only just organised it about half an hour ago."

"We already hang out once a week," he whined.

Marina looked him over as she stood up. "I don't care either way. Do what you want."

"Then I choose to hang out with Lottie."

Marina looked between us with a smile. "Of course you do."

Not knowing what that meant, we said our goodbyes to her.

The next weekend, Alex insisted we go on a shopping mates date from the comfort of our window seat.

"Why?" I asked.

"You need a dress."

"I'm sure I have something at home I can wear. I'll get Mum to photo everything I have and send it."

"When was the last time you went to a wedding or a formal?" he asked me.

I thought about it. "I was seven."

"Was this an older man situation, or…?" he teased.

I threw a cushion at him. "It was a wedding. Not mine!" I said quickly before he could make another joke. "My uncle's."

He nodded. "Right. Now, I know you're not exactly a big person…but have you, maybe, grown since then?"

"Mum and I are somehow shopping online together…in like five minutes, can't I just get a twofer dress?"

"Oh, good idea!" Alex said brightly. "Although, that might require showing your legs."

I frowned. "Why would it require me showing my legs?"

He shrugged. "Guests don't usually wear floor length dresses to weddings, do they?"

"How am I supposed to know?"

Alex looked at me for a second. "Good point."

"You could at least pretend to argue."

He threw me a grin as my Skype started ringing on my laptop. "Why? You'd just argue then. Way easier to agree with you."

I didn't know if I loved that or hated that.

"Hey, Mum," I said as I answered the call.

"Hi, Mary!" Alex called, hovering over my shoulder.

"Hi, Alex," Mum said with a smile.

"I hear we're dress shopping!" Alex said happily.

"You coming, too?" Mum asked.

Alex settled himself on the window seat beside me. "I was going to take her shopping for a dress for my brother's wedding, but–"

"Oh, that's nice. Lottie says I need to return a form about that?"

Alex nodded and angled the computer to himself. I flailed my hands and sat back until I was needed.

"Yep," he said. "There's a form for leaving mid-term with another student. Super easy, takes like five seconds. It just needs to be my name and for two nights. The Friday to the Sunday."

Mum was clearly writing things down on a pad next to her keyboard. "Okay. And that's in…three weeks?" she asked.

"Yep."

"Is your aunt driving you?"

"She is, yes."

"Oh," Mum said, presumably to me. "Your own mini field trip with the principal!"

I rolled my eyes. "Can we get on, please?"

"Sure. I found two websites I think look good," Mum said.

"I don't doubt you did. What are they?"

Mum squinted at the screen. "JJ's House and…ASOS."

"Oh, ASOS!" Alex said happily.

I looked at him.

"What? They have good stuff."

Mum dropped the links in the chat section and I opened them up.

"Are they going to ship in time?" I asked.

"Yes, they'll ship in time. Although, we wouldn't have this problem if you'd just told me about this over the holidays," Mum said pointedly.

"Yeah, yeah. I suck," I muttered as I started scrolling through the websites.

"Oh, that one's nice," Alex said.

I glared at him. "What's with the giant slit up it? I don't need people seeing my knees."

"It's hardly the Regency, Lottie," Mum said.

"I'm aware of that, but what's the point of a long dress just to have a great big gash–"

"Moving on, then," Alex said, taking over the scrolling. "How do you sort on this?"

He and Mum basically took over, sharing dresses back and forth. While they were busy with the first site, I opened up ASOS on my phone and scrolled through that to see if

252

there was something that caught my eye. Most of it looked way too casual to suit the formal, but one thing did jump out at me. It wasn't something I ever thought I'd like, but there it was.

"This," I said, sitting up.

"What?" Mum asked.

I spun my phone to the camera. "Can you see it?"

"Where's it from?"

"ASOS."

"What is it?"

I typed the name of it in the chat and we waited a few minutes while Mum looked for it.

"Lemme see?" Alex asked, holding his hand out.

I passed him my phone. He looked at the picture, then looked at me, then looked at the picture. Finally, he smiled.

"I think you'd look awesome in that."

So did I. It was a pale pink thing – a colour I could pull off even with the red-head in me – thin straps, a-line with a flared skirt, and what looked like hundreds of fake petals all over it. It looked feminine, but grunge-able at the same time.

"Oh, you could pair it with your boots," Mum said,

obviously thinking the same thing as me. "Make it more you. Do you have your boots?"

I nodded. "I've got my boots."

"And your black cardy?"

I nodded again. "Like I'd go anywhere without my black cardy," I scoffed with a smile.

"Well, that was easier than I expected," Mum said happily, sitting back in her chair and picking up a glass of wine.

"You're telling me," Alex said, almost mimicking Mum's pose, just minus the wine.

After a few sips, Mum leant forward again. "You guys are room 605?" she asked.

"Yep," Alex answered.

"What are you doing?" I asked.

"Ordering this dress," she said. "You can't wear it if we feel so pleased with our find that we forget to actually buy it."

I nodded to Alex. "She's a thinker."

"She is," Alex laughed.

"So, I guess I'm wearing a dress," I said, sighing in resignation but actually kind of looking forward to it.

Chapter Twenty-One

Driving with Ms Wilson or, as Alex called her, Aunt Tam was not as terrifying as I'd first expected it to be.

Firstly, she had very similar taste in music to Mum so I recognised a bunch of the songs she played. Secondly, when Alex complained about the music selection, the first thing out of her mouth was, "Driver picks the music, shotgun shuts his cake hole". Anyone who quoted 'Supernatural' had to be okay, right?

I sat in the back seat, mostly content to listen to Alex and Tamara – which she'd insisted I call her as soon as we left school grounds – chatting and laughing, or staring out the window and pretending I was riding a horse alongside the car. A weird thing I'd done since I was very little.

I'd thought arriving at Acacia had been an awe-inspiring sight? Arriving at the Landrys' winery was nothing short of spectacular, especially as we'd arrived after dark and the place was set up for a wedding. Fairy lights were strewn everywhere; though trees, around pergolas, across the driveway. The whole place was lit up and it was magical. If this was the way the Landrys did weddings, I could get on board.

"All right, warning time, Lottie," Tamara said as we came up to a more homely looking house. "My sister is a bit…"

"Insane?" Alex muttered.

"I was going to say intense," Tamara said as she pulled to a stop. "She's a perfectionist."

"That's putting it mildly," Alex said as he hopped out of the car.

Tamara swivelled to look at me. "I'm sure he's explained his relationship with his parents is…tense. It means a lot that you're here with him for this."

I suddenly felt that my presence meant a whole lot more than I'd realised. It didn't freak me out, and for a second it felt like it should, but it humbled me.

I nodded to her. "Thanks."

As though the serious moment was now over, Tamara nodded. "All right, let's go and face the horde."

We both got out and I saw Alex was being greeted by a bunch of people on the verandah. Tamara smiled at me as we made our way over.

"Just wait until you try the cake!" a guy who looked a lot like Alex, but older, was saying to him.

"Have you lost weight?" a woman asked him. "I don't know what we'll do if your tux doesn't fit."

"Sylvie!" Tamara called, pushing her way into the woman's arms.

"Tam, there you are," she said. Then pulled away from her sister and looked to Alex. "Aren't you going to introduce us your friend?"

His friend was more than happy to just sit in the shadows and not be noticed by anybody, but that seemed like it wasn't going to happen.

"Why don't we get inside first?" Tamara asked. "Where's Loz?"

Alex gave me a reassuring smile as Tamara ushered everyone else inside and left just the two of us outside.

"Doing okay?"

I nodded. "Fine."

"I forgot how much social interaction this was going to be for you."

I smiled at the sentiment. "All good. I'm just here for you."

I held my hand out to him and he took it before leading the way inside.

The noise was immense as he led me down the central hallway.

It was a double-fronted cottage, the kind Mum had always wanted. Left and right were rooms, some doors closed, some open. We walked past a staircase leading upstairs and another presumably to a cellar. Finally, the hallway opened out into a huge, obviously modern open plan living area, complete with fire place.

"There he is!" a young woman cried.

"Hey, Loz," Alex nodded as she came over.

She looked at me with a big smile. "This must be Lottie. Hi. I'm Eliza. Alex's soon to be sister-in-law. Everyone calls me Loz."

I gave her a smile back. It was only polite. "Nice to meet

you. Congratulations."

She grinned. "Thank you. Come and meet the others."

Loz got between Alex and me and guided me over to where everyone had congregated around the fire with glasses of various libations.

"Everyone, quiet. Quiet for the bride," Loz called.

There were amused titters that suggested she was taking the piss a little.

"Right, thank you. Everyone this is Lottie, Alex's new friend from school."

There were varied choruses of "Hi, Lottie," from those gathered.

Loz nodded approvingly. "Now, this is Ilya, my husband-to-be."

Ilya, the guy who looked like older Alex, came over with a nod. "Thanks for coming."

I nodded. "Thanks for having me."

"This is Ed, Alex's dad. His mum, Sylvia. Wonderful woman. You know Marina. And, this," here she steered me over to the corner to a stern looking older woman, "is Babushka."

Babushka looked me over and I couldn't tell if she

approved or not. Suddenly, my usual librarian-with-a-dash-of-grunge look felt rather inadequate.

"This is Elliott?" she asked, with a slight accent, and I nodded.

"Yup, I'm Elliott."

Babushka gave me another once over, then stood up. I'm woman enough to admit I swayed backwards in lieu of taking an actual step backwards. But I needn't have worried. Babushka suddenly grinned widely and pulled me in for a huge hug.

"Welcome to our home."

So, obviously, not all Alex's family were causes of tension. That or they played a really good game.

"Why don't you show her to your room?" Ilya asked Alex. "Maybe give her the tour?"

Alex nodded, oddly quiet and somewhat withdrawn. "Sure."

Alex held his hand out for mine and I took it. As he led me back out of the room, I bumped his shoulder gently with mine.

"You okay?" I asked him.

He sighed as he pushed out the front door and looked

up at the stars. "You know how you go home every holidays?"

I nodded. "Yeah…"

"Yeah, it's more like I leave home." He ran a hand over his chin. "To come here."

"I'm sorry."

He gave me a sad but grateful smile. "It is. I just…it's hard coming back. Especially now Ilya's in Adelaide with Loz and Marina's usually at uni or off somewhere for Mum and Dad. I mean, I've got Babushka, but she doesn't want to hang out with her teenage grandson all the time. Woman's got shit to do." He squeezed my hand. "Anyway, enough sulking. Let me show you how the Landrys do an event."

He brightened as we got closer to the space set out for the wedding and showed me around. There was the wedding arch and all the chairs set up in one refurbished barn. Then another bedecked in tulle and set up with tables and chairs for dinner. There was room for dancing and a bar. More fairy lights twinkled everywhere the eye looked, bathing us in a warm glow.

As we stood on the dancefloor, Alex spun me around

and pulled me to him as though he were going to start dancing.

"I didn't know you danced," I laughed, my arm around his neck.

He swayed us gently. "I don't usually. But Mum and Dad taught us when we were little. I've forgotten how to do a proper Waltz, but I remember the basics."

I smiled as we side-stepped around for a bit. I was feeling warm and fuzzy inside, seeing this slightly different side to my friend. It was nice we were close. It was nice to have his hand in mine. It was nice to feel the warmth of his body radiating onto mine.

Finally, he let me go and said, "Come on. Next stop."

"There are stops?"

He nodded as he dragged me out of the barn. "It's the grand Landry tour. Well, not the full tour. That would take hours on foot. I'll take you down to the cellar door and show you around on Sunday."

Alex showed me his favourite tree and the dam where he and his siblings caught yabbies when they were younger. He showed me his fort and the stream with the tire swing where he broke his arm when he was ten.

Finally, we dropped down into a pile of hay and watched the stars, our hands still joined.

"This place is awesome," I breathed.

"It's not so bad when there's someone to share it with." I could hear the smile in his voice.

I shook my head and looked at him. "No. I mean it's awesome. It's perfect. And there's only minimal people. Don't tell me you have a library, too."

"We do have a library, actually."

"It's like paradise."

He laughed. "When the cellar door's closed, yeah. I always feel slightly…on display when it's open. Even though they normally don't come up this far."

He turned his head to look at me.

"Bugger. And here I thought I'd found my happy place."

He squeezed my hand. "It's happy when you're here."

I squeezed his back, feeling that little burst of happy in my chest.

"Alex! Lottie!" we heard someone call. "Dinner's ready!"

Alex sat up and ran his hands through his hair to

dislodge the straw he was obviously expecting was in it. "Come on. I'll show you my room on the way in."

"Your room?" I asked sceptically, wondering why Ilya and Alex both mentioned me seeing Alex's room.

He nodded as he helped me up. "You'll be staying in there. I'm on the futon in Dad's study."

I wrinkled my nose. Alex pulled some straw out of my hair. "That doesn't seem fair."

"All the guest rooms are full up. Besides, it's comfy enough."

We headed inside to dinner, via his room. Tamara had already put my bag and dress in there for me.

It looked nothing like his room at school, where there were trophies and posters and all manner of just…stuff that gets accumulated by living. It was stark and bland, like it had fallen out of a homemaker catalogue. I didn't wonder so much why he felt more at home at school.

Dinner with his family was a noisy affair full of overlapped conversations – predominantly about wine that I could barely follow, let alone add to. Loz's parents and maid of honour were there as well, adding to the fray. His parents did seem a bit...aloof, but I could also feel more love at that table than Alex had led me to expect.

Chapter Twenty-Two

Saturday disappeared in last-minute preparations.

Loz, her family and maid of honour were staying down in the B&B near the cellar door so we didn't see much of them, but the Landrys were in full 'totally not panicking' mode almost as soon as the enormous, boozy breakfast was over.

Ilya couldn't find his cufflinks, but they turned up in Sylvia's jewellery box.

Alex's buttonhole was temporarily lost but found in the back of the wine fridge.

Ed's tie had a stain on it, so he had to find another one.

Sylvia's shoe strap broke, which meant she had to wear a different pair of – to me identical – nude heels.

Tamara, Babushka and I sat out on the terrace dressed up in our finery – them sipping Mimosas and me with orange juice and lemonade – in an effort to keep out of the way.

Finally, all the kinks had been sorted and we traipsed down to the ceremony barn.

Where there had been empty fields the night before, were row upon row of cars.

Since Alex was in the bridal party, I was put into Tamara's capable care. Which was promptly taken over by Babushka.

"There's Edward's mother," she said to me, indicating a woman at the other end of the aisle we sat. I could tell exactly what she thought about Alex's paternal grandmother in those three words.

"She's retired to a nice little place down the road," Tamara explained. "Ed and his brothers have been running the place since their dad died."

"Tractor accident," Babushka said knowingly.

I looked at Tamara behind Babushka's head and knew my eyes were like saucers. Tamara grinned and shook her head. I had a feeling, the more I got to know her, the more

I was going to like Babushka.

The ceremony was beautiful…says every guest at any wedding. It wasn't wrong, but I only had one to compare it to, and everything from my uncle's wedding kind of faded after I'd been let loose on the lolly bar.

Now and then, Alex would find me and give me a smile. He did look very dapper up there with his tux and his hair for once not sticking up but lying flatter. The resemblance to his brother was even more stark with them both dressed up like that.

After the ceremony, the guests wandered into the other barn while the bridal party and family had photos. I was a bit lost during that bit, since I didn't feel like I really belonged to either group and I was loathe to move too far away from people I actually knew. I think Loz saw this. I saw no other reason for her to pull me into the last few pictures.

Tamara and Babushka took me into the bigger barn to find our table while the bridal party made their entrances. I thought Alex looked quite young next to his sister all done up. It was adorable.

Alex had to sit at the bridal table but, after dinner was

eaten and the cake was cut and the first dance was danced, he came to find me. His cheeks were flushed and I wondered if his brother had been slipping him some celebratory drinks. Babushka had certainly tried that on me. I'd had a half glass of champagne and my brain felt like it was fizzing merrily.

"Sorry," he said as he held his hands out for mine. "I thought I could get to you between entrée and main, but Ilya kept me busy."

I smiled as he hugged me. "All good."

"Not too much social interaction?"

I shook my head as he pulled back to look at me. "No. Babushka's been telling me stories and Tam's been correcting them behind her back."

Alex laughed. "Sounds about right. Good stories I hope?"

"Mainly about your dad's side...?" I ended it in question as though I needed clarification.

Alex snorted. "Oh, yeah. Babushka *hates* them. No idea why. I think she just likes to be old and eccentric."

"Don't we all," I said wistfully.

"My two favourite people are getting on well, then?"

I nodded, feeling that little burst of happy. "Yes."

"Good. Dance?"

Usually, dancing in public would have been a firm no, hard pass, ask the next girl. But I was feeling very unusual so I nodded.

Alex pulled me onto the dance floor and we boogied on down until we were both in desperate need of a drink from too much exercise in a cramped space and too much laughing for absolutely no reason.

"Coke? Lemonade? Water?" he asked me as I fell into my seat.

I only had the energy to nod at that point.

He laughed, "I'll be back in a tick."

Then Marina dropped into the chair next to me with a drink of her own.

"You didn't have to bring a date?" I asked her.

She grinned around her straw. "No. I did. He's probably off banging one of the bridal party."

I didn't quite know what to say to that, but she waved her hand at me.

"Max and I have an…understanding," she chuckled. "He comes with me to all the boring family events, keeps

270

Mum off my back, and he can have at any guest unwitting enough to fall for his salacious charm."

I nodded. "Sounds like fun."

Marina laughed. "He is. But not until you're older."

I shook my head with a smile. "No. I didn't… I'm good, thanks."

She looked at me the way people look at you after they've had a couple of drinks and they think they're about to drop something profound on you.

"Because you like my brother."

I snorted. "What?"

She nodded. "And he likes you."

"No."

"Yes. Don't care what you two say, I'm a believer."

"What do you believe?" Alex asked as he came back.

"You two like each other."

Alex and I looked at each other like stunned mullets for a moment, then both burst into laughter, with much shaking of heads and words to the negative.

Marina got up, nodding a lot. "Yes." She waved her finger in the air. "You'll see. I need another drink…"

And she wasn't the only person we had to disagree with

271

over the course of the night.

"You make a good addition to our family, Elliott," Babushka said to me later and I packed out in giggles.

I exchanged a look with Alex as I tucked my hair behind my ear. "Oh, no! It's not…"

"Lottie and I are just friends, Babushka," Alex finished for me.

She looked down at his arm around my waist. "Are you now, Sasha?"

His arm left my waist and instead picked up my hand. "Good friends, but just friends."

We exchanged another, warm smile.

Babushka muttered something in what I assumed was Russian, then walked away.

"So, people think we're dating," Alex said, humour in his voice.

I leant into him for a second. "I wonder what gives them that idea?"

"I don't know."

"It's crazy."

"Madness," he agreed and we both laughed.

It was good to laugh with Alex. It was easy. It was like

an undeniable force took hold of me when we were together. I liked it.

"Come on, let's get out of here," he said to me, pulling me towards the doors.

"Ilya won't miss you?"

He shrugged. "I doubt it."

He took me out to a clear patch of grass and wrapped his arm around my shoulders. I put mine around his waist. And we just wandered and talked long into the night. Even after the music in the barn had been turned down and most of the guests had left.

"Do you know anything about the stars?" he asked me.

I looked up at the sky. "Not really."

He chuckled and kissed my temple. "Something the great Elliott Hopkins doesn't know."

"The stars never really interested me. Maybe if I lived out here and I saw them so brightly every night."

"It's pretty amazing, isn't it?"

The moon was full. Alex stopped us and put his other arm around me.

"You know what I think when I'm here and you're at home?" he asked.

"No," I said as I leant against him. "What?"

"That even though we're not together, if you looked at the moon and I looked at the moon, we'd be looking at the same moon." He shook his head. "I swear that sounded less stupid in my head.

I appreciated the sentiment, so I hugged him tightly. "I get it. That's nice."

He pulled back to look at me and brushed a stray curl off my face. He was so close, his nose brushing mine. I almost wanted to stay in the moment forever.

But, when it started raining lightly, we decided it was time to call it a night and ran for the cover of the house, laughing all the way. My feet slipped a little on the verandah and Alex caught me easily, our gazes lingering for a few moments before he walked me to his room.

As we paused in the doorway, he leant on the frame next to me. Our bodies were close enough that mine was on high alert for the slightest touch, accidental or not.

His fingers played with mine. "I actually enjoyed myself at *home* for once, E. Thank you." The way he said 'home' made it all the more obvious how he felt about the place.

"I had a really nice time. Thanks for asking me to come with you," I said as I tucked my hair behind my ear.

Our eyes met and I saw behind the humour is his. Behind the easy, carefree guy he was in the school halls. Behind the guy who just wanted to be liked and get along with everyone. I realised it wasn't the first time I'd seen it. Not by a long shot. Had I really been paying attention, I would have noticed it far sooner. Far more often. I would have noticed he was always himself with me.

"I'll see you in the morning," he said quietly.

I nodded, feeling a soft smile on my face as I looked at him. I watched as his answering smile fluttered to life. It wasn't the only thing that fluttered.

"Good night, Alex," I said so quietly it was more a whisper.

For the span of mere seconds, the gap closed between us and our lips met in a simple, brief, warm kiss that left a wider smile on my face.

"Night, Lottie," he said before giving my hand a gentle squeeze and heading off to his bed.

I hurried into his room, closing the door behind me and leaning on it until the sudden flurry of activity in my chest subsided. My fingers brushed my lips softly. My lips, where his had just been. There was something so terrifying and yet so…not about what had just happened.

The not part, somehow, seemed the most frightening.

Chapter Twenty-Three

Alex and I went back to Acacia and things went back to normal. Which is not to say that things were ever not normal. They were. Always normal.

We'd kissed.

So what?

It clearly didn't mean anything.

Alex had met me the next morning with a friendly shoulder bump and we'd both gone on as though nothing happened so well that I thought maybe I'd dreamt the whole thing. After all, I'd been giddy with the atmosphere and half a glass of bubbles.

I decided not to dwell on the kiss and just move on, as Alex was clearly doing.

When I headed for the bathroom on Monday morning, Alex was coming out of it.

So much for not wandering around in just a towel anymore, but at least he was holding it in place as our bodies bumped into each other with nothing more than my flimsy PJ tee between us.

Not that I noticed.

Nor did I notice his hand on my hip or my hand on his naked chest.

Nope.

Didn't notice.

"Hey," he chuckled. "My bad."

I shook my head. "No. All me. Sorry."

We stood there for a few moments and my brain had no idea what it was thinking. I did decide, though, that the tremble in my tummy was just hunger uncharacteristically early in the day.

"You going to breakfast now?" I asked him.

He looked down for a second. "I *was* going to get dressed first…"

"Probably a good idea. Wouldn't want the girls of Acacia to lose their minds so early in the day."

278

As he flexed his muscles, he gave me that crooked smile I couldn't help but return. "Huh?" he asked, waggling his eyebrows. "But, seriously. It's not like they don't see it plenty."

All humour I felt rushed out of me. "Oh."

He smirked. "Swimmer. Remember? Those budgie smugglers leave *very* little to the imagination."

"I've never seen you swim," I said suddenly, trying not to think about him in his budgie smugglers very hard.

He shook his head. "You haven't. We've got a comp coming up in a couple of weeks here at home. The boys will love to have someone new to use their boring old material about the visiting team on."

I nodded. "Sure. Sounds good. I'll be there."

"Cool." He made to head to his room. "Why did you ask about breakfast?"

"Oh," I said. "I was going to ask you to wait."

"Elliott Hopkins, having breakfast…" he teased. "What has the world come to?"

"Sasha Landry, wearing clothes…" I mimicked his tone and he grinned.

"Be quick. I'm starving after that practice."

279

I was quick. Weirdly quick. 'Aware not to keep him waiting' quick. It was most unlike me.

On Tuesday, things were still normal.

Normally normal.

I didn't think about our kiss as we sat on the floor of the library and nudged each other back and forth while we pretended to do homework.

On Wednesday, the same.

Alex and I were sitting at Lunch with the boys and I stole one of his chips, like usual.

He turned to berate me and then broke into a wide smile.

"What?" I asked.

"You've got..." he said, shaking his head with an exasperatedly fond smirk. "Here."

He then proceeded to wipe some sauce off my face and lick it off his finger.

My heart thudded in my chest. My cheek tingled where he'd touched it. But, in answer to his split-second grin, all I had was a smile.

On Thursday night, while we watched tellie, we held hands until he stretched his arm around my shoulders. Had I been thinking about the fact we'd kissed, I wouldn't have snuggled into him and let us both get more comfortable.

On Friday, I accidentally fell in his lap while I was trying to manoeuvre around Zac to get to a place on the couch. His hands went to my hips and his nose brushed my cheek as he laughed.

"You good, E?" he asked.

I nodded. "Fine. Just navigating the jungle of legs you boys have."

His hands tightened ever so briefly on me, like he didn't want me to move. For a moment. I didn't want to move. But I had to move because I couldn't just sit on Alex's lap forever.

On Saturday, he was showing me a funny cat video on his phone on the window seat.

"Did you see the…" he laughed as we turned to look at each other.

We were so close, his nose bumped my cheek.

We looked at each other and I felt my stomach tumble and my chest flutter.

"I thought you'd like it," he said softly.

"I did. Thanks."

Then he was shifting over and on his phone, leaving me

to get back to my reading.

On Sunday, he pulled my chair out for me at dinner and kissed my cheek as I sat down.

The other boys chuckled and teased him, but he sat down with a shrug.

"What?" he laughed and I felt him touch my leg briefly. "You can't kiss a friend's cheek?"

"Let me check," Fret said, then leant over and kissed Luke at the same time Zac leant in from the other side to kiss Luke.

Luke winced, then smiled. "Better than I expected."

"You think I'd bite you or something?" Zac asked.

Alex leant towards me and whispered in my ear, "Sorry."

I shook my head and whispered back. "Don't be."

We looked into each other's eyes and I felt the connection to him. The thing that joined us now. I couldn't imagine my life without him in it anymore. He'd barrelled into it uninvited and, quite to my surprise, I didn't want him to leave.

Which definitely didn't make me wonder where our kiss featured into it.

I realised, by the amount of time I told myself I wasn't thinking about our kiss, that I was lying to myself. I wondered why that was. Was I holding back from him? If I was, why was I? Was I just convinced he'd never see me as anything other than a friend? Or was I more worried he'd see me as something else?

The questioning myself was exhausting.

Alex had stated on multiple occasions that we were just friends and he'd been believable every time. With me. With his sister. With his babushka.

I wasn't scared he'd see me as more than a friend.

I was sure he saw me as just a friend.

The problem was, I wasn't sure I saw him as just a friend anymore.

Chapter Twenty-Four

"Angelsharks! Angelsharks Angelsharks!" the people around us cheered and I laughed.

"Do people seriously get riled up about this stuff?" I asked.

"When we play against Preston College, yeah," Birdman said as he looked around the pool.

I'd been led to believe that Preston College were our closest rivals. Teams from Preston came to Acacia, or vice versa, for an intercollegiate match or tournament for every available sport.

It wasn't in the Australian spirit to wave school scarves around at sporting events, but you could tell who the Acacia kids were when Alex Landry stepped up to the block.

"Why Angelsharks?" I asked as everyone around us roared.

"Species in Australia," Luke said. "All the sports' teams are named after one. Rugby's Rock Wallabies."

"Baseball's Bandicoots," Zac said.

"Basketball's Bilbies," Birdman added.

"Soccer's…Sugar Gliders," Fret finished resentfully.

I snorted. "No. I'm sorry. That's unfortunate."

"The Angelsharks are by far the best team–" Birdman started.

"Especially now Alex's hit his stride," Zac interrupted.

"The rest of us don't announce it quite so loudly," Birdman finished.

"Frisbee Fruit Bats," Fret offered.

"Seriously?" I asked.

All of them nodded.

"Oh, yes," Fret said.

"That's more unfortunate than the Sugar Gliders," I said.

Fret nodded. "Oh, yes."

Zac shook my leg. "Alex is up. Alex is up!"

"Settle down, fanboy," I teased, but I was feeling pretty excited myself.

It was time to see what all the fuss was about.

And, boy did I get more than I bargained for.

Alex stood on his block at one of the centre lanes. Even under the swimming cap and goggles, I knew it was him. I'd recognise that toned body anywhere. Not that he was wearing much more than a swimming cap and goggles. He'd been right. Budgie smugglers left NOTHING to the imagination.

Nothing.

Not a single thing.

But my brain did its darndest to prove them wrong anyway.

He swung his arms and stretched his neck the way I'd seen swimmers do at the Olympics. Now and then he nodded to someone to one side of him or the other.

"Yeah, Alex!" Zac suddenly boomed out, standing up and throwing his arms in the air.

Alex didn't react.

"Alex!" Birdman joined him.

Alex still didn't react.

286

"Woo!" Fret stood up as well.

Still, Alex didn't react.

I shrugged, stood up, cupped my mouth with my hands, and yelled as loudly as I could, "Come on, Alex!"

Even from a bit of a distance, I saw the curl of his lips into a smile as he got into position.

"Which race is this?" I asked the boys, feeling myself smiling.

"100m Freestyle," Birdman answered.

"Ooh, there's that arsehole from last year," Luke said.

"What arsehole?" I asked.

"Middle lane next to Alex." He paused while the gun went off and the swimmers launched into the pool. "He was the only guy Alex couldn't beat last year. The only one."

"That dick beat him by a second in every race," Zac said.

"So there's kind of a lot riding on this?" I asked.

Luke nodded. "That's an understatement."

It seemed useless to cheer Alex on while their heads were mostly under water, but we did it anyway. And, despite there being numerous Angelsharks in the pool,

287

Alex's name was being chanted the loudest.

I didn't even really know how swimming worked. Was there some sort of trick or rule to it? But my heart was in my throat as Alex and the arsehole from Preston were pretty well tied the whole way.

Alex sheared through the water like a man on a mission. His arms gliding powerfully. He was a thing to behold and I regretted it was the first time I'd seen him swim.

In the final lap, the cheers rang out even harder and I tried to make sure he'd hear my voice among the noise. Slowly, Alex started pulling ahead.

Barely visible to the naked eye, Alex's hand hit the end of the pool before the arsehole's.

"Did he do it?" I asked the boys.

"He did it!" Zac yelled.

"Alex won!" Luke laughed.

"Of course he did," Fret said. "Alex is the best."

It wasn't the only race Alex won. Every race he was in, he won.

He kicked butt in the Butterfly.

He led his team to victory in the Relays.

He sent the Preston boys packing in the Breaststroke.

He just scraped through in the Backstroke.

By the end of the competition, my voice was raw from cheering him on so loudly, but I was busting with pride.

The boys and I clapped as he was given his medals and awarded the intercol trophy.

As he held it aloft, he looked at me and beamed.

The pool started emptying of spectators and the Preston people, but Alex came over to us.

"You won!" I exclaimed as he wrapped me up in a hug, neither of us caring he was still wet from his last race.

"I won!" he cried happily. "I won!"

There was much cheering and celebrating the whole way to the locker rooms, where I waited outside. I could hear them all shouting and laughing.

After a couple of minutes, Birdman came out.

"Alex said he's gonna head up to the dorm and change, and we should go ahead to the party."

I nodded. "Yes, the party. Where are the others?"

"He is the champion!" Fret was singing as he came out of the locker room with the others.

And he kept singing, making up a lot of the lyrics to suit Alex and his wins…and just generally making up lyrics in lieu of all the parts of the song he didn't know. Which was most of it.

The Banksia rec room had been bedecked in green and grey with the Angelsharks image strung up and a banner that read 'Congratulations' across it.

"What were they going to do if they lost?" I asked.

"We had another banner," a random kid said as she walked by.

I nodded. "Good to be prepared."

Zac and Fret sussed out the food table while I waited for Alex to arrive.

But when we hadn't seen him for forty-five minutes, I started to worry something was wrong.

"I'm going to go up and see what he's up to," I said to Birdman over the noise of the party.

He nodded. "Good idea."

I squeezed my way out of the overfull room that was surely bordering on a health and safety violation, and hurried up to our dorm.

I swung around the doorframe to Alex's room. He was sitting on his bed with his phone in his hands.

"Hey, there you are," I said and he looked up.

"Hey."

"Everyone's missing you downstairs."

He nodded. "Just had to report back to the family."

I walked in and sat next to him. "I'm proud of you."

He looked at me, a small smile at his lips. "Thanks, E."

I bumped him. "I'm serious. I heard you were good, but you were *good*. And I know absolutely nothing about swimming," I said as though I was a complete authority.

He laughed. "It meant a lot you were there. Again."

I shrugged. "That's what friends do, right?"

I put my arms around him and gave him a hug. He just seemed like he needed a hug. Based on the way he hugged me back, my assumption had been correct.

"You good?" I asked him.

His nose was in my neck and it was giving me goosebumps. I felt myself lean into him more, and him into me. Then, we were pulling away, him giving my temple a kiss on the way past.

But, when we were looking at each other, our arms didn't drop. Alex's had one hand on my waist and the other rested on my leg. I had one arm around his neck and my other hand was on his chest. Our eyes search each other's faces as though committing them to memory.

"Lottie?" he asked quietly.

"Yeah, Alex?"

My eyes darted down as he licked his lip, then I was kissing him. Or he was kissing me. Kissing was occurring. Unlike after his brother's wedding, this wasn't the briefest of tiny kisses. Sweet though that had been, this was something else entirely.

This was hungry.

This was heated.

This was full of all the words I wouldn't – or couldn't – say.

He still smelled vaguely of chlorine, lingering despite his shower and liberal application of deodorant. He was warm. Sure. Secure. Safe.

In that moment, I forgot we were just friends with definitely no benefits.

That moment seemed like the most perfect place to be.

Alex's hand tightened on my hip and mine slid into his hair.

"Alex! Alex! Alex!" came the chant from the living room.

Alex and I pulled apart slowly, returning to some semblance of normal just before Zac and Fret barrelled into his room.

"There you guys are!" Fret shouted excitedly.

"There is a party downstairs with your name on it," Zac announced. "And by party, I mean cake."

Fret elbowed him. "And he can't eat any until you show your ugly mug."

"He also can't."

"Hence, hurry up!" Fret said, throwing his arms in the air as Zac came to haul Alex off the bed.

"Uh, I…" Alex said, looking at me.

So many unsaid things rushed between us. So many things that I couldn't – or wouldn't – let myself think.

"No time for dawdling, 'cos you are the champion…of the pool!" Fret sang as he started pulling Alex out of the room.

"But, Lottie–" Alex started.

"Is coming, too," Zac promised, holding his hand out for me.

Alex's eyes were pleading for me to come with or come up with an excuse for him to stay and for them to go

293

without us.

He wanted to talk.

I didn't.

What would I even say?

'Sorry I can't keep my lips off you. I'm the worst just-friend ever'?

"I'll be there in a second," I said to them.

"Lottie!" Alex called as Zac and Fret hauled him out of there.

I wasn't just a second.

Unless you count the time it took for me to get to my room and close the door behind me.

Chapter Twenty-Five

I avoided Alex for as long as I could.

I could no longer deny it. I liked him. As in more than a friend liked him. As in, I'd kissed him twice and would quite like to do it again. A lot.

Having lost the ability to reject this notion any longer, I wasn't quite sure how to act around Alex anymore. My brain stopped and didn't know what to say when he asked me simple things like 'What do you want to watch?' or 'You need another cup of tea?' No answer seemed like one that wouldn't give my secret up.

I remembered what Alex had said about secrets. How it was difficult to keep them in close quarters. Well, this was one secret I'd take to my grave if I had to. Further than that, even.

Except for two kisses, Alex had showed no signs of reciprocating my feelings, so I laboured under the assumption that he still just wanted to be friends. Whether he thought benefits could be included now or not, I didn't know, but I sure as hell wasn't interested in that sort of deal with him.

So, I just had to work through this weird little crush I'd developed. It would go away with time. Surely. Then we could go back to being just friends again.

My friend, though, had other ideas.

It was impossible to avoid him completely, especially when he started staking out the living room anytime he thought I was likely to pass through it. And that day was no exception.

"Lottie!" Alex said.

I gave him a nod and tried my best to hurry to my room as fast as I could while looking as casual as possible. My knee hit a side table, which gave Alex the time he needed to leap over the couch and block the door to my room.

"All right," Alex said in a 'brook no argument' voice. I'd never heard him sound so cool, calm, confident, authoritative and serious. "This is stupid."

I looked up at him. "What's stupid?"

He scoffed, "What's stupid?" He paused for a second. "What's stupid? Elliott, really?"

If he was pulling out the full names, I could do that too. And play dumb with the best of them. "I don't know what you're talking about, Sasha, but I have homework I need to do."

"Your homework can wait. We need to talk."

"About what?"

"You know what about. This whole thing is ridiculous. We have to talk about it. I'm not going to let a couple of maybe misguided kisses ruin one of my best friendships."

I blinked. "Misguided?"

He nodded. "Look. I get it. Lines blur. It doesn't have to mean anything, that's okay. We can just put it down as tried and move on. You mean too much to me not to work this out."

I was suddenly inexplicably angry with him. Or with me. Maybe with both of us. "You don't get it do you? You in this ivory tower where nothing touches you." I pushed him in my frustration, but knew it wasn't his fault. "It's already ruined. I ruined it. I broke my promise."

Now Alex was blinking. "What? What promise?"

My hand went to push him again, but ended up just lying on his chest. "I broke my promise. I…" I owed it to him to look him in the eye when I smacked that final nail in the coffin. "I like you, Alex. I'm sorry. I broke my promise and I fell for you anyway. And I'm sorry I've been ignoring you since… You know. I just couldn't…" I petered off as he'd started laughing.

One of his hands curled around mine on his chest as his laughter burbled through him.

"Yeah. All right," I muttered self-consciously. "I know I'm an idiot." I tried to extricate my hand from his, but he held it tightly.

I finally looked up at him and his other hand brushed over my cheek. "I'm not laughing because you're an idiot. I'm laughing because… Well, we're both idiots. You're not the only one who ruined it and broke your promise. I broke my promise, too, E."

It took me a good few seconds to work out what he was saying there. Him saying what I thought he was saying just didn't compute. He was the guy who never fell. He was the

298

guy who protected his heart against anything and everything like his very life depended on it.

"I like you, too, Lottie," he said softly. "Like, *like* like you. I couldn't help it. I don't even know when it happened. One minute we were friends, the next I was trying to convince myself I didn't really want more."

"But you do?"

He nodded. "Yeah."

"You want more with the future swamp witch?"

He smiled and took a step towards me. "Future swamp witches can't have kept men?"

"Oh, kept men," I laughed. "You're not planning on doing any work then?"

He shrugged. "Of course I will, but making and selling wine is hardly going to be as important as whatever you decide to do."

"Flattery might get you everywhere, Sasha," I warned him.

He laughed.

"Besides," I added, "don't try that on with my mum. Pretty sure she thinks making and selling wine is more important. Especially selling it to her."

"Girlfriend's mum doesn't have to pay."

"You haven't seen how much my mum can drink."

"I'm willing to risk it."

We just stood and looked at each other for a moment.

"Girlfriend?" I finally asked him.

He huffed self-consciously and ran his hand through his hair. "Uh, yeah. Maybe. I hope. If you want?"

"Is that what you want?" I asked him.

He smiled softly. "I've spent enough proper time with you to know I like you, Lottie. To know that I want to spend a lot more time with you."

"What happened to the guy who was worried about Birdman breaking my heart so I never talked to any of you again?"

"Ah. If you recall, I'm also the guy who believes life is for living and risks are for taking. Besides I was jealous and just really didn't want you to hook up with him."

"You were jealous?"

He nodded. "I like you enough to risk our friendship, Lottie. I like you that much. The optimist in me just really hopes that, if it doesn't work out, we can be civilised about it."

"What are we? Seventeen going on thirty?" I teased him.

He smiled. "What do you think?"

What did I think? I'd thought it was just me. I'd thought I'd just gone and ruined our friendship and broken our promise. I thought things were just going to be a bit awkward until I got over it, but I was willing to work through the awkwardness because, as much as I liked him, I didn't want to lose him. If we could get through a couple of presumed embarrassing kisses and ~~love~~ like believed unrequited, then...

I had to hope we could get through anything.

Maybe it was wishful thinking because I really wanted to give us a go. Maybe it was his never-ending optimism rubbing off on me. Or maybe it was actually possible.

I was going to go with hope.

"I think I agree," I finally said to him. "I think I want to be your girlfriend."

He grinned as his hands went to my waist and we took a step closer to each other.

"Yeah?" he asked, his forehead resting on mine.

I nodded against him. "Yeah."

Our lips got closer as I suddenly thought of something.

"No!" I said quickly, my hand on his chest.

"No?" he asked, sounding confused and hurt.

"The formal!"

"What about it?" He shrugged. "It'll be easy for me to get a tie to match your dress."

I shook my head. "No. The guys. We said we were going stag."

"So?"

I shoved him gently. "So, Fret cancelled on Kayla because *you* insisted. You can't then turn around with a date."

"Who said I wanted to go with you anyway?" he teased.

I smirked. "Oh, so now you don't want to go to the formal with your girlfriend?"

He laughed. "Maybe I don't."

"We can't tell them, yet."

"What? Why not?"

"Because they'll feel like…" I did some quick Maths in my head and it got too complicated. "All the extra wheels."

Alex's face suddenly dropped all humour. "Will they?"

"Won't they? It'll be hard to convince them we're not

going to the formal *together* if they know we're dating. I don't want to ruin our plans."

Alex nodded. "Okay. True. Maybe. So, we wait until after to tell them?"

I nodded. "Yeah. Okay. Sounds good."

Alex opened his mouth, paused, held up a finger and said, "Does that mean I'm not allowed to kiss you now?"

I smiled. "You can kiss me now."

He gave me one of his infectious smiles. At least, it would have been infectious had I not already been beaming myself.

This time, our kiss was warm and sunny and made me think that fireworks might really exist. Our arms were around each other and I wasn't worried about what it meant or if we were ruining our friendship. I just leant into it, into him.

He made me feel all the warm and fuzzy feelings inside.

He made my heart flutter and my tummy tie itself in excitable knots.

But he also made me laugh.

He made me happy.

He made me want to trust and love blindly.

We could share jokes and movies and ice cream.

We could sit in perfect silence, on opposite ends of the room, and I was grateful he was there.

With him, I didn't care about social interaction. I could spend every hour of every day with him and not get tired of it. Well, almost.

Part of me was wary about what would happen with my new-found friends if this didn't work. But I could easily ignore it because I didn't think my roommate was a mistake at all.

Chapter Twenty-Six

Week eight and the formal was finally here. Alex, at least, was excited. I thought it was a little bittersweet since I was moving into one of Callistemon House's newly renovated dorms before the end of term.

I wasn't looking forward to being in a new place all over again, especially potentially by myself, but there was also a massive difference between rooming with your friend and your boyfriend.

Alex kissed my neck and I pushed him away.

"They'll be here any minute," I hissed.

He laughed. "So?"

"So we're pretending we're not dating because you convinced them all to go stag with us. This is not a date,

Sasha, therefore hands off."

He held his hands up with a laugh. "All right. Dating five minutes and you're already bossing me around."

As I put in my earring, I looked at him. "It's been more than five minutes, and I've always bossed you around."

He nodded in agreement. "Fair."

"Now, go away and let me finish getting dressed."

He looked me over critically. "Dress. Shoes. Hair. Makeup. Aren't you done yet?"

I heaved a sigh of exasperation and ushered him out of the bathroom. "Begone before I burn you with the straightener," I said as I brandished it at him.

He burst into chuckles and I closed the door on him.

We'd always had the unspoken rule that a closed door meant 'bugger off', while an open door meant 'you can come in and do other open door related activities'. Thus far, it only included teeth brushing and hair styling, and I was in no rush to add anything else to that list.

By the time I felt done, the boys were lounging in the living room in their tuxes.

"Wahey!" Zac cried when he saw me. "And you said you didn't scrub up nice."

I swished my skirts in a rare display of coquettish playfulness. "I turned out okay."

"Okay?" Birdman scoffed. "You look beautiful, Lottie."

"You think so?" I asked, not one to scrounge for compliments but totally one to beg for reassurance that I wasn't hallucinating.

Birdman nodded. "I think so."

"Me too," Fret said.

"Lovely," Luke agreed.

"I think 'wahey' covered it best," Zac added and we all laughed.

"Shall we crack on?" Alex asked, looking at me with a smile in his eyes.

I felt like the belle escorted to the ball by five strapping, dapper lads. I'm pretty sure that's what I looked like as well. Not that anyone was about to think I'd collected myself a harem of athletic lovers or anything. Not after seeing me hang out with them for most of the year.

As we walked into the Hall – reserved for full-school assemblies and fancy functions like formals – we had our picture taken as a group, me in the middle as one of the shortest.

The Green and Grey was a sit-down dinner event, so we found our table. Conveniently, Kayla and a couple of her friends were also at our table. I looked at Birdman.

"Did you do that?"

He shrugged. "I may have known someone who could swing it."

"Oo, you've got people for everything, do you?"

"Need to kill a man?" he asked. "I know a guy."

I snorted. "Sure, Mr Bond."

He and I shifted the name cards on the table so that Fret and Kayla were sitting next to each other, then sat back and watched as they thought it was a coincidence.

As I watched them talking, I thought of something. "You know, you never told me why he's call Fret."

Alex laughed as he sat next to me. "You want to tell it?" he asked Birdman. "Or, shall I?"

"You do it."

"Right," Alex said. "So, in Year 8, we're all these little piddly things. Rock up for Day 1. Don't know anyone. We've got PE. Somehow a bird gets into the locker room where we're all changing. No one wants to admit it's kinda of scary, with it all swooping and flapping and shit. Anyway, this tiny little dude with this squeaky arse voice goes, 'Don't fret!'. The whole room packs out laughing and the legend of 'Fret' is born."

"What happened to the bird?" I asked.

"You know," Birdman said. "I don't remember."

"Mr Hill shooed it out with a broom," Zac said, his mouth full.

"Where did you get that?" Alex asked.

Zac pointed. "Tiny food table."

"You mean *hors d'oeuvres*?" I clarified.

Zac nodded. "Yep. Them." Then he noticed Fret sitting next to Kayla. "Oi," he said, kicking his head to Birdman. "You do that?"

"A gentleman doesn't meddle and tell," Birdman said.

Zac rolled his eyes. "I'm getting more food."

We sat through dinner, chatting and laughing. We took pictures. So many pictures. There was dancing. There were balloons. It was a great night with great friends. It made me miss Flick and Leah and Marsh a bit, realising that I'd never get to do this with them after all the years of friendship.

So, I sent them a picture of me with all the boys and captioned it 'wish you were here'. I felt my phone buzz a few times after, but knew that they'd wait until morning. But, I resolved, no longer. I'd been slacking in the friendship department with them that year and was determined to make up for it going forward.

Had Alex and the boys somehow infected me with some of their extrovert tendencies?

Maybe that wasn't such a bad thing.

Later on, Alex and I snuck away to get a picture of the two of us but, when we were done, we noticed that all four of the boys were standing there waiting for us.

"Something you two would like to share with the group?" Zac asked.

By the looks on their faces, they already knew what the something was.

"All right," Alex said, bringing them all I close. "Lottie and I are dating."

There was a collective sigh of relief.

"What's that supposed to mean?" Alex asked them.

"We have been trying to get you two to admit you like each other for weeks," Birdman said.

310

"Weeks?" said Fret. "Try months."

"All that malarky with the condom," Zac sighed.

"How did you two not notice it was the *same one*?" Luke asked. "It honestly didn't take a genius to work it out."

"How would *you* know it was the same one?" Alex asked, indignantly.

Fret smirked. "We marked it. Checked on it now and then. We had bets going."

"Who was going to actually use it," Birdman said.

"Who'd notice it had a Sharpie star in the corner," Luke added.

"How long it'd keep changing hands," Zac added.

"Hey," Birdman said. "You guys can use it together now."

"Naw," Fret said with a little clap of his hands. "How poetic."

Alex and I exchanged a glance that was clearly a silent gag.

Although, I had to admit that I felt pretty good that he wasn't actually sleeping with as many girls as his condom requirements had suggested.

"You weren't sleeping with other guys?" Alex asked me.

I shook my head. "And you weren't sleeping with other girls."

He shook his head as well. "No."

"He's still a virgin," Birdman hooted.

"Like you boys aren't," I scoffed.

"Ah," Zac said. "But we're not the ones who pretended we were sleeping around just so we could deny our feelings for the one person we actually wanted to sleep with."

Alex thumped him as he cleared his throat. "Yeah. All right. Thank you."

I snorted. "When you put it like that…"

Alex looked up at the ceiling. "Mistakes were made, Elliott. Idiocy occurred. Can we move on, please?"

"Hey," I said, willing to put my dignity aside to make him feel better, "it's not like you were the only one."

When he looked at me, his face brightened. "True. You were also an idiot."

I exchanged a look with the other boys and we all laughed.

"Sure, Sasha. I was also an idiot."

"Does this mean I can go and spend some time with Kayla?" Fret asked, his hands clasped together.

"Yes!" I told him. "Yes. God. And apologise to her again!"

Zac waved a hand as Fret dashed off. "They grow up so fast."

"I'm sure he knows how to make it up to her," Birdman said and Luke shoved him.

It was like nothing had changed.

Nothing except now Alex held my hand and it meant something different than before. Something bigger. Something more. Something that felt like it had been there all along.

Chapter Twenty-Seven

I still couldn't believe it.

Alex was nothing I thought I liked in a guy. But then, we got along so well it kind of made sense I'd fallen for him at the same time.

The fact we'd both been hiding behind pretend hook ups was hilarious and it made me feel better to know I hadn't been the only one who'd done it to make sure my behaviour couldn't be misconstrued by either of us as romantic. Instead of making me wonder if that meant we weren't really suited, it made me feel like we were. We'd both put our friendship first. We'd both put what we thought the other one wanted first. And if that wasn't a good sign, I didn't know what was. It did, though, make me more resolved to be better at communicating in future so we didn't have any more stupid, easily avoidable misunderstandings.

The renovations to Callistemon House were finally finished and they found me a brand spanking new room a week before Term Three finished. It was weird to go from the hustle and bustle of Banksia House to the relative quiet of Callistemon House. Very few people were moved given there wasn't really that much time left until Christmas, so it wasn't a surprise when I ended up without a roommate for the rest of the year.

It would have been lonely, which was something I wasn't used to feeling after so many months in Banksia Room 605, but the boys popped by unannounced more often than not. It probably said more about my introvert tendencies that I just holed up in my room and assumed they'd come find me if they wanted to hang out instead of going to find them. It probably said a lot about their extrovert tendencies that they were perfectly happy to come and find me without a second thought.

Alex came and visited me and Mum in the holidays for a whole week.

I took him to all the typical haunts; Rundle Mall, The Parade, Glenelg. We did touristy things, forcing me to experience my own home city in new and exciting ways. It wasn't like Alex had *never* been to the city and hung out before but, when it was usually for competitions, there wasn't an awful lot of time for exploring.

I almost thought having him in my house for a week would be annoying, but I found that it was actually quite similar to the way we'd been living for the previous eight months. After a few weeks without it, I was surprised to find I'd missed it.

We tried to keep our relationship on the downlow, thinking it was probably a bit early to be letting the adults in on it after they'd let us share a dorm for nearly three whole terms. Last thing they needed was to be worried about shenanigans. I don't think we were totally successful, but Mum didn't say anything about it either.

Term 4 was full on.

There were exams.

Zac was back into baseball.

Birdman was back into basketball. And basketball meant I was reminded of Zahra. So I wheeled our way to one of the girls' games to watch her.

"I heard they broke up," I said to him.

He nodded. "I heard that, too."

"So…?" I prompted.

He grinned. "So maybe I don't want to be a rebound guy."

"You basketballers and your fancy terms," I teased and he laughed.

"Pardon the pun."

"So, you're not going to ask her out?"

He rubbed his chin. "Not this year."

"Why not? A lot can happen in six weeks!"

He nodded. "Exactly. What if I ask her out, she says yes, then over Summer she forgets why she said yes and breaks up with me before we've even really had a chance?"

"Wow," I breathed. "You've really thought this through."

"Why?" he chuckled. "What did you and Alex do?"

"Uh," I took a second to recall. "We got all jealous. Both pretended we were sleeping around to avoid suspicion. Kissed pretty much by accident. Twice. Then I didn't talk to him which made him really grumpy and we kinda argued until we realised we both wanted to date?"

It was his turn to say, "Wow."

"Yup." I nodded. "We didn't think about it at all. In fact, had we spent less time actively not thinking about it, then we might not have made such a mess."

"Could be worse," he said.

"How's that?"

"He could have just been pissed with you, not made you both confront your feelings, then you'd be in Callistemon all by yourself and we'd all have lost you."

"Ugh," I muttered. "Don't remind me what could happen if this doesn't work."

Birdman shook his head. "Too late now."

"For what?"

"If you guys break up, we're gonna draw straws to work out who gets to be friends with who." He grinned at me cheekily.

"Really?"

"Well, that's what we've said."

"I'll bet no one wants me, though."

He snorted. "Everyone wants you."

"Instead of Alex?"

"Ideally, we won't have to choose."

I nodded. "That would be ideal."

Which I did realise could be my way of saying I hoped or wanted Alex and I to be together forever, but my brain didn't have the capacity to think that far ahead at that point. I saw no current future where I didn't want to be with him, and that was enough. For now.

"Remind me why we're at the girls' basketball match?" Alex said as he sat next to me on the bleachers.

I looked at Birdman and failed to hide my smile.

He sighed heavily. "I've got a bit of a thing for their point guard," he said.

Fret hooted. Although, he could talk. Him, holding hands with his girlfriend who had, thankfully, not held a grudge that he'd ditched her to go stag with me and the others.

"Aw," Kayla said. "Zahra's sweet."

"Don't tell her!" Birdman said.

Kayla mimed sealing her lips. "I won't."

"How long have you liked her?" Zac sang.

"Like…all year," Birdman admitted.

Alex whacked him. "So, why haven't you asked her

out?"

Birdman shrugged. "I'd never really talked to her. She was dating Angus Curry–"

"Now she's broken up with Angus Curry," Alex finished for him. "So why not ask her now?"

"Next year," Birdman promised.

"And if she finds someone else before then?"

"Then it wasn't meant to be."

"I really don't approve of the healthy outlooks you guys have," I said.

"I agree," Kayla said. "It's kind of unnerving to find well-adjusted teenagers."

It was nice to have another girl in the group who was as self-deprecating and sarcastic as I was.

"She's a keeper," I told Fret as I pointed to her.

He was bursting with joy. "Yeah, she is."

"You're a keeper," Alex whispered into my ear.

"Mushy much?" I laughed.

I felt his smile against my cheek. "Sometimes, that's allowed."

I turned to him. "All right. I'll allow it."

"Good."

I kissed him. At school. In front of who only knew. Where anyone could see.

Because we weren't roommates anymore. We were dating.

It was weird.

It was wonderful.

It was.

And I wasn't going to worry about things I didn't want to change.

Epilogue

The next year when I walked into Acacia Academy, I felt like a markedly different person than the one who'd first seen those hallowed halls.

Not only did I have actual friends that I could barely go five minutes without talking to, I had a bona fide boyfriend. And a 'captain of the swim team', 'happy to get up at the arse crack of dawn', 'falls asleep during most movie nights' boyfriend to boot.

Not being new meant I arrived directly to my dorm like all the other old hands. Mum and I hauled my suitcases up to my dorm room in Callistemon House. There was no way I could room with Alex that year. It would be a little against school policy given that our relationship had been rather hard to hide from Aunt Tam over the Summer holidays. Especially when Mum and I had been invited to the Landry's winery for New Years' Eve.

"Well, this is nice," Mum said as she looked around.

I'd shown her pictures of the new room, but she always liked to see the real thing.

"Not as nice as your dorm with *Alex* though, I'm sure," she finished and I rolled my eyes at her.

She'd found it utterly hilarious that Alex and I had ended up together. Her words were, "Only something in a romance novel," as she giggled gleefully the whole way back home to Adelaide at the end of the previous year.

I knew what we looked like and I didn't care. I really liked Alex. I might even love him. Almost. If seventeen-year-olds could be trusted with knowing anything about love.

"Yeah, yeah," I muttered to Mum. "My room's this one."

I pushed my way into my room, dragging my suitcase awkwardly behind me. Mum followed suit. I'd left a few things behind the year before. Sheets, pillows and doona covers I didn't need at home. My school shoes, which had been a total accident. Library books I'd meant to take back before Christmas. Bits and bobs I thought I could last the summer without.

"Cleaning this all up at the end of the year is going to require a moving van," Mum teased.

"Har har," was my retort. "You should see Alex's room."

"Hello?" voice called from the living room.

I pushed my way passed Mum to see who my new roommate was going to be. I was surprised to see I recognised her. Long, dark legs. Wavy brown hair. A smile that lit up any room she walked into.

"You're…" *Do not say Birdman's crush!* "Zahra, right?" I asked with a smile.

She nodded. "Yeah. It's Lottie?"

I nodded. "It is. I mean, I am."

I'd heard so much about Zahra from Birdman that I felt a little like I was crushing on her myself for a second.

"Nice to meet you," she chuckled. "Which room's mine?"

I pointed, but before I could get any words out, two boisterous boys barrelled into the living room, chanting my name.

"Elliott! Elliott! Elliott!" Zac seemed most pleased with himself, but Birdman's voice cut out with a squeak at the sight of Zahra.

Birdman's eyes shot to me in panic as Zac cried, "Where is your boyfriend? He's late."

Zac then stopped and took in the room. "Oh, hey, Birdman! It's Zahra."

Birdman looked like a roo caught in headlights, but he nodded. "Yep," seemed all he was capable of saying.

Zahra didn't seem fazed at all. "Henry Bird, right?" she asked him, like she was surprised to see him of all people in her dorm room.

Birdman nodded again. "Yep."

"You're a point guard, too, yeah?"

One more nod. "Yep."

Zahra smiled at him warmly. "Cool. I didn't know you were friends with Lottie."

"Best of friends," Zac said happily. "But just friends. She's dating Alex."

Zahra smiled even wider. "I had heard that."

"Birdman's single," Zac continued, only to be thumped

by Birdman.

"You guys pop by a lot?" Zahra asked.

I nodded. "They do. Sorry. I can tell them not to?"

Zahra's smile for Birdman was a different sort of smile now. "No. Don't do that. It's totally fine."

"Oohhh…" Zac started, only to get thumped again.

"Party in Callistemon!" Fret yelled as he, Luke and Alex appeared.

I looked at Zahra. "I am so sorry."

She smiled. "Don't be. I'm always up for a good time."

"I warn you," Fret said as Alex came over to say hi to me. "I am *very* good fun."

Luke whacked him.

"How was your drive?" Alex asked, wrapping his arms around my waist.

"Good. You?"

He nodded as he kissed my cheek. "Good. Ready for another whirlwind adventure year at Acacia Academy?"

I looked at our friends.

I looked at Birdman, then Zahra.

If I'd thought the previous year was going to be

interesting, this one had the potential to be even more so.

"This is going to be fun." I smiled at him.

the Art of Breaking Up

If you like *the Roommate Mistake*, you might also enjoy my concurrent release, *the Art of Breaking Up*.

Wade Phillips shattered Lisa McGinty's heart in Year 10 for no known reason. One minute he was the perfect boy-next-door boyfriend, star goalie on the soccer team, and future head prefect. The next he was like a different person altogether.

Lisa and I were used to his sarcastic teasing, his shallow taunting, and his insincere flirting. My best friend put on a brave face in front of him, but she still felt the sting. I knew she still loved him. At least, she thought she did. I kept waiting for her to see he wasn't worth it.

No one knew what happened to Wade and no one got close to him anymore. Not until a life-altering incident throws me unavoidably into his path.

For one single second, I see through the armour he's built. It takes just one single second for him to see through mine. Something connects us. It turns out, Wade Phillips might be the only one who understands me. It turns out, I might be the only one who understands him.

Wade Phillips might be the guy to teach me the art of breaking up, but will my heart – and Lisa's – break in the process?

Buy in print and eBook now: https://books2read.com/u/bpzpBE

the Roommate Mistake

Thank you so much for reading this story! Word of mouth is super valuable to authors. So, if you have a few moments to rate/review Lottie and Alex's story – or, even just pass it on to a friend – I would be really appreciative.

Have you looked for my books in store, or at your local or school library and can't find them? Just let your friendly staff member or librarian know that they can order copies directly from LightningSource/Ingram.

If you want to keep up to date with my new releases, rambles and writing progress, sign up to my newsletter at https://landing.mailerlite.com/webforms/landing/y1n6q2.

You can find the playlist for *the Roommate Mistake* on Spotify:
I also have a generic writing playlist you can check out 😊

Follow me:

Thanks

Is it over? Did I do it?

Time blurred with this one. I was fighting two infections and some serious sleep-deprivation. Still, I think I ended up with something pretty good. I like it anyway and, as the proverbial They say, you've got to write stories you want to read.

Thanks to the beta team for keeping me accountable and checking in on me when you hadn't heard from me for a while. You guys go a heck of a long way to keeping me to my deadlines. I still don't know what I did to deserve such an awesome crew and I thank the powers that be for you every day.

Thanks to those people who ARC reviewed *the Art of Breaking Up*. Those reviews were crucial in reminding me I do know what I'm doing and I am actually a good writer. And I had A LOT of crises of faith through writing this one with all the ups and downs.

I do want to apologise to those people who pre-ordered the print version and ended up with the wrong book because my distributor printed them early. If you've not got it sorted and you see this, please email me a pic of the mismatched insides and we'll work out how to get you the right copy.

And finally, I'd like to thank my husband, obviously. You're one of my kind and my life would suck without you.

My Books

You can find where to buy all my books in print and ebook at my website; www.elizabethstevens.com.au/.

About the Author

Writer. Reader. Perpetual student. Nerd.

Born in New Zealand to a Brit and an Australian, I am a writer with a passion for all things storytelling. I love reading, writing, TV and movies, gaming, and spending time with family and friends. I am an avid fan of British comedy, superheroes, and SuperWhoLock. I have too many favourite books, but I fell in love with reading after Isobelle Carmody's *Obernewtyn*. I am obsessed with all things mythological – my current focus being old-style Irish faeries. I live in Adelaide (South Australia) with my long-suffering husband, delirious dog, mad cat, two chickens, and a lazy turtle.

Contact me:

Email: contact@elizabethstevens.com.au
Website: www.elizabethstevens.com.au
Twitter: www.twitter.com/writer_iz
Instagram: www.instagram.com/writeriz
Facebook: https://www.facebook.com/elizabethstevens88/

CPSIA information can be obtained
at www.ICGtesting.com
Printed in the USA
LVHW092110120621
689906LV00012B/99